BLOOD VINTAGE

A FOLK HORROR NOVEL

J.F. PENN

Blood Vintage. A Folk Horror Novel

Copyright © J.F. Penn (2024).

First Edition Special Hardback ISBN: 978-1-915425-68-3
Paperback ISBN: 978-1-915425-69-0
Large Print ISBN: 978-1-915425-70-6
Ebook ISBN: 978-1-915425-71-3
Audiobook ISBN: 978-1-915425-72-0

www.JFPenn.com

Requests to publish work from this book should be
sent to: joanna@JFPenn.com

Cover and interior images generated by J.F. Penn on DALLE and Midjourney with commercial license

Cover and Interior Design: JD Smith Design

Published by Curl Up Press

www.CurlUpPress.com

CHAPTER 1

"NATURE OVER GREED!" THE motley crew of eco-warriors and environmental activists shouted as they rattled the bars of the high metal gates, chanting slogans in a chorus of anger and defiance.

Rebecca Langford turned her back and tried to ignore them, huddling into her down jacket as an icy wind sliced through the construction site. It was unseasonably cold for April, and the grey skies and vicious weather did nothing to improve the mood of her fellow workers. Her team was already behind schedule with the new housing development on the northern edge of London, and the delays were multiplied by the protestors who made every day a struggle.

The determined activists sought to protect the last trees of an ancient woodland from being cut down. Many wore camouflage gear, their clothing a patchwork of green and brown that reflected the natural world. Some carried climbing harnesses and ropes as they readied themselves to take action.

But it was their headgear that set them apart from the usual mob.

Their hats and helmets were adorned with twisting vines, leaves, and branches. Some even had horns, and their silhouettes took on a bestial, almost demonic aspect in the pale light. It was as if the ancient trees had summoned a legion of half-human, half-animal warriors who had come to claim the last vestiges of this sacred place for their own.

Rebecca shook her head to clear the vision. These were just ordinary people, idealists who believed passionately in their cause. But something about them, something primal and otherworldly, sent a shiver down her spine that had nothing to do with the cold. There was a wildness in the air, a sense of barely contained chaos that threatened to spill over at any moment.

She pushed down the sense of foreboding. The protestors were behind strong gates, and the clearance must be done today. They couldn't waste any more time.

Rebecca looked down at the architectural plans she had designed many months ago as she considered the next steps.

Her original designs had incorporated a line of the most ancient trees at the edge of the forest, allowing them to remain intact, but the upper echelons of management insisted on making the most of every metre of the land they owned. Somehow, they received planning permission to take down the last of the ancient forest. Nature must make way for progress, as it had done in this city for millennia, and the government had mandated new housing, even at the expense of the green belt. This place, once a sacred boundary between civilisation and untamed forest, was now deemed a necessary sacrifice.

But Rebecca's job was to build for the future of the people who would live here once the housing site was done, the thousands who flocked to London every week, with their ever-growing need for more space. Over the last few weeks, most of the ancient wood had been reduced to a barren wasteland, its majestic trees now nothing more than lifeless stumps and shattered branches littering the muddy earth. Today, the last of the trees would come down.

Rebecca tugged her hard hat down more securely on

her head, finding a kind of security in its protection as she signalled to the group of workers ready to tackle the trees.

One man seated in a bulldozer nodded and began to drive forward, inching slowly toward one of the ancient oaks.

The massive tread of the machine churned the earth, grinding and tearing at the ground as it approached. Its metal teeth, jagged and merciless, tore into the wood with a sickening crunch.

The tree shuddered, the wood creaking and groaning at the bulldozer's relentless assault. Its blade ripped into the heartwood. Branches cracked off, lying on the ground like twisted, lifeless limbs. Other workers collected the debris to throw into the wood chipper, and the acrid scent of sap with the bitter tang of smoke from the machine rose into the air.

The protestors roared their fury.

"Murderers!"

"Bastards!"

They rattled at the metal gates, their cries almost drowned out by the roar of the bulldozer. Rebecca's heart thumped in her chest at their fury, but she clenched her fists inside the sleeves of her jacket and bit her lip, holding her nerve as she tried to ignore the rising threats.

She had to get this done and prove she could handle the difficult aspects of the job away from the office. It was the only way to get ahead in the fiercely competitive world of corporate architecture, and she needed the change that new opportunities would bring.

A sudden creak came from behind her as the metal bars of the fence twisted and screeched along the concrete.

Rebecca spun around.

A group of protestors surged through a newly made gap. Others climbed over the gates and raced toward the bulldozer and the ancient trees.

The driver saw them coming, dropped out of the cab, and ran for the safety of the site hut. The protestors swarmed over the machine, attacking it with wrenches and crowbars, breaking glass, denting metal.

A young man threw himself against the trunk of the ancient oak, only inches from the heavy metal blade of the bulldozer. He wrapped his arms around the gnarled bark, his fingers scrabbling for purchase as he fumbled with a length of chain. He looped it around the tree and then around his own waist, his movements frantic and desperate.

One of the other construction workers lunged at the protestor. "Get the hell away!"

The two men grappled and slammed against the tree with a sickening thud. The protestor cried out in pain as his head banged against the blade of the bulldozer.

Blood welled and dripped down the bark of the ancient tree, crimson drops seeping into its crevices as if the oak itself were bleeding.

The protestors surged forward.

A group of them swarmed the construction worker, their fists and feet lashing out in a frenzy. The worker fell to the ground, his hard hat tumbling from his head as he tried to shield himself from the onslaught of blows. His cries of pain and fear mingled with the shouts of the protestors.

Rebecca felt a surge of panic rising in her chest, her heart pounding as she stood frozen in the midst of the violence exploding around her. She wanted to help the fallen worker, but what could she do against so many?

The sound of sirens cut through the noise.

The site manager shouted above the chaos from the doorway of the site hut. "The police are on their way! They'll be here any minute."

His words rattled the protestors. They left the injured worker lying on the ground and turned back to the trees, the imminent arrival of the police driving them to their original purpose.

A young woman with ivy wound through her matted

dreadlocks pulled out a tube of industrial glue, smeared the adhesive on her hands and clothes before pressing herself against the smooth trunk of an enormous beech tree. An older woman, her silver hair cropped elfin short, wrapped a chain around her waist and secured herself to an oak, then sat down, arms crossed, ready to face the authorities.

Two young men climbed the biggest tree, finding purchase on the gnarled branches as they ascended into the canopy and attached themselves with a combination of ropes and mesh that would be difficult to untangle.

And everywhere, the glint of phones held high, cameras live-streaming the destruction. Every brutal detail, every splash of blood, every twisted branch.

More protestors surged through the gap in the fence now, joining their comrades in widening circles around the trunks, some sitting, some lying down. They covered themselves with branches, daubing their clothes and skin with red paint as if they were corpses, dying to protect the ancient forest.

Rebecca noticed a young woman who bent to help another protestor chain herself to a trunk. Her profile was so familiar.

Rebecca's heart skipped a beat, and for a moment, the world around her faded into a muted blur. The determined set of the woman's shoulders, the dark curls wound with flowers… Could it really be Grace?

Her sister had been a passionate eco-activist and when she vanished five years ago in rural Somerset in the west of England, the police implied that her radical militancy had led her into trouble, or that somehow her alternative lifestyle and bad choices meant she deserved whatever happened.

The sisters had been close once, united by a shared love of nature and a desire to make the world a better place. But as Grace's activism grew more radical and uncompromising, the rift between them had widened. By the time Rebecca moved to London and started at the architecture firm, they hardly spoke anymore. Grace's disappearance officially remained a cold case, but Rebecca had never lost hope.

She pushed through the crowd, her eyes locked on the woman by the tree as she shoved past angry protestors and confused construction workers. Her breath came in ragged gasps as she drew closer.

The woman turned towards her. For a heart-stopping moment, Rebecca was certain it was her sister, but as she reached out, her fingertips grazing the woman's sleeve, the illusion shattered.

Up close, the differences became apparent. It wasn't Grace, just another protestor caught up in the fury of the moment.

Rebecca's heart sank, the desperate hope that buoyed her now replaced by a crushing sense of disappointment and loss. She was suddenly exhausted, her energy draining away, leaving her almost boneless.

A protestor shoved a phone in Rebecca's face, the camera lens close to her nose. "Murderer! You did this!"

Rebecca recoiled at his fury. As she turned to run, he slammed something into her chest.

The blow was sharp, a stabbing pain, knocking the air from her lungs. She clutched at her chest.

Her fingers came away red and dripping.

CHAPTER 2

THE PROTESTOR REARED BACK, a triumphant smile on his face as he held his phone out, filming her shocked reaction.

Rebecca gasped for breath even as she realised she wasn't injured. It was just red paint, now splattered across her chest like a gout of blood.

"You're killing the earth. Murderer!" the man shouted as he threw another paint balloon.

It exploded against her shoulder and splattered her face.

Rebecca spun away and half ran, half stumbled through the crowd.

Her vision blurred with tears as they jostled her, their elbows and shoulders slamming into her body as she fought to get to safety.

She tripped, nearly losing her footing on the churned earth, but managed to catch herself at the last moment.

With a final, desperate surge of energy, Rebecca broke free from the crowd and raced towards the site manager's hut. As she made it to the door, her colleagues reached out to pull her inside.

Rebecca sank to the ground, her back against the wall, her legs leaden as adrenalin pulsed through her system. She took deep breaths, trying to calm her heart rate.

One of the workers brought her a mug of hot, sweet tea. "Drink this, love. It will make you feel better."

The site manager, Alan, was on the phone, his brow furrowed and his voice tense.

"Yes, they've broken through. One man is badly hurt. We need an ambulance as well as the police."

He turned to look at Rebecca, his eyes widening at the splatter of red paint on her chest and her face. "You okay?"

"Not really. I need to clean up."

"Go home," Alan said, his voice gruff, his brow furrowed. "We can't continue, not with this lot inside the site. We need to get them moved on before we can get back to work. The bastards look like they're well-entrenched now. Bloody hippie tree huggers."

Sirens blared from outside as the police arrived, the officers well used to dealing with eco-protestors. As they processed the scene, an ambulance pulled up and the injured worker was helped inside.

Rebecca went into the bathroom and used paper towels to daub as much of the paint off as possible, but it was matted into her hair and stained her skin. Her clothes were ruined. The only thing she wanted to do was go home and close her curtains and shut out the day.

She pulled on her coat and tugged it around her to hide the worst of the damage, then slipped out the back of the hut.

As she hurried to the Tube station, leaving the onslaught of the protestors' shouts behind, the last of the red paint dripped down off her shoes, leaving a trail of crimson drops on the pavement behind her.

Rebecca descended into the depths of the Tube station, and as the train pulled up, she stumbled aboard, her legs giving way as she collapsed into a seat.

It was typical of London that no one said a word about her dishevelled appearance or the spatters of red on her skin.

The unspoken rule: Keep your gaze neutral and unfixed on anything or anyone; avoid getting involved.

Rebecca closed her eyes as the events of the morning played out in a relentless loop. The sound of wood cracking, the shouts of protestors, the accusation of murder, the fake blood. It all swirled together until the rocking of the train became unbearable.

She swallowed down the nausea, counting the stops until she reached her destination.

Rebecca finally emerged from the depths of the Tube station. She stood for a moment, grateful for the chill spring air as she leaned against the wall, breathing deeply, waiting for the nausea to pass.

Her phone, which had been mercifully silent underground, suddenly erupted with a cacophony of messages and missed calls.

She unlocked the screen and scrolled through the barrage of messages and texts, her heart beating faster at the sheer volume — and then the graphic threats of violence from unknown numbers.

In the last hour, it seemed the video of her confrontation with the protestor had gone viral. It had been expertly intercut with earlier images of her giving the signal to cut down the ancient trees. She was portrayed as the villain, solely responsible for the destruction. The video was spreading fast across social media, and had been picked up by news media, further amplifying its message.

But that was only the beginning.

The eco-activists had already doxxed her. Her name and photo, and worst of all, her home address and phone number, were plastered across video platforms and messaging apps, websites and forums, calling for vigilante justice against those who would destroy nature.

Rebecca's phone rang, the shrill, insistent tone cutting through the din of the city streets. An unknown number flashed across the screen.

She declined the call.

It rang again — and again.

She switched it to silent, then noticed a message from Alan, her manager.

> I've seen the video. Take some leave and get away from London until this dies down. It's not safe for you here right now.

His words cut through her overwhelm. She had to get away.

Rebecca pushed away from the wall of the Tube station and hurried back towards her flat, the implications of the text sinking like a lead weight in her stomach.

Her home was no sanctuary now. She had to get out of the city and find somewhere safe to hide until the storm blew over.

But where could she go?

London had once held so much promise, so much potential, but now it felt hard and unyielding. She had put everything into her work, and for a time, it seemed like it was worth it. When things were going well, London was a bright place of endless possibility, but when the shadows lengthened, it was easy to become one of the nameless lost in darkness, too quickly forgotten.

The city burned through the potential of its inhabitants and drained the vitality from those who walked its streets daily. London demanded everything from those who loved it and gave little in return. Those who left it exhausted rarely returned.

In truth, Rebecca had no real friends here. Acquaintances and work colleagues, for sure, but no one she could ask for help. There had been occasional lovers, brief flings and one-night stands, but no one she would even want to call in this situation.

And her parents… well, they were a half a world away.

After Grace's disappearance, they had thrown themselves into charity work, burying their grief in the refugee camps of the Congo. They had left England, seeking solace in helping those who suffered even greater tragedies than their own. Her parents had sold the family home when they left, as if trying to purge their collective history along with memories of Grace.

The recollection of her sister's vibrant smile, of the easy way she had with people, made Rebecca's breath catch in her throat. Grace would have been on the side of the protestors today, but she never would have hurt her sister. She could have run to Grace and been welcomed with open arms, whatever trouble she was in. But that was not an option now.

As Rebecca reached the high-rise flats, the streets seemed to close in around her. Tower blocks of grey concrete and steel loomed overhead, and it was even colder in the shadowed places where the sun never reached.

The housing estate was a dreary, lifeless place, a monument to the triumph of functionality over form. It offended her architectural sensibilities, but it was all Rebecca could afford. The blocks of flats were identical, the facades a patchwork of drab, weathered concrete and peeling paint. The only splashes of colour came from the occasional graffiti tag, a futile act of rebellion against the crushing monotony of urban life.

There were trees planted in neat rows along the edge of the pavement, but they were bricked in and cemented in place. Controlled by the sprawling city. There was no wildness here, no untamed beauty, and Rebecca suddenly had a glimpse of what would replace the ancient trees at her own building site. She had tried her best to design something with movement and natural flow, but those with the money had crushed her best endeavours, saying it was too expensive. Now she was painted as the enemy.

She reached her flat and fumbled with the keys, her hands so cold and trembling that she almost dropped them. Finally, the lock clicked open, and Rebecca stumbled inside. She stood for a moment, her back against the door, on the edge of crying at the relief of being away from the street.

Her flat was tiny and cramped, a far cry from the airy, light-filled homes she dreamed of designing. It was hers — but it wasn't a sanctuary any longer. She couldn't stay here.

Rebecca checked her phone. There were now hundreds of messages and calls. She would just delete them all, and she would certainly not check social media. It would be filled with hate and graphic violence, and she couldn't deal with that right now.

She just had to pack a bag and get out of here.

Rebecca quickly changed out of her paint-stained clothes and shoved as much as she could in a backpack, assuming she'd be gone for a few weeks at least.

She paused by her desk, drawn to the photograph in a silver frame. A glimpse of a happier time. She and Grace stood arm in arm as they laughed together against the verdant backdrop of rural Somerset in the southwest of England, where Grace had worked at the time.

Her sister's hair reflected the sunlight, and her hazel eyes sparkled with joy. Around her neck, she wore a carved pendant made of reclaimed wood featuring the triple moon, representing the maiden, mother, and crone.

Rebecca reached out and touched her sister's face with a fingertip. Grace had always been the brave one, standing up for what she believed in, no matter the cost. Rebecca needed that courage now more than ever.

Distant shouts came from outside, then a chant that she recognised from the site earlier. "Nature over greed!"

The protestors were coming.

Rebecca grabbed the photo and shoved it into her backpack. She dashed out the door, double-locked it behind her, and headed for the passageways behind the estate.

She raced through the maze of stairs and only slowed down when she was far enough away that she could no longer hear the noise of the protestors. She pulled up the hood of her jacket as it started to rain, grateful for the anonymity as commuters hurried past, heads down.

The turn in the weather would hopefully keep the protestors away from her flat, and if she was lucky, a new target would soon take the heat from her. She might not need to be away too long, but she still needed a destination.

As she navigated the streets to a Tube station further away from her flat, Rebecca thought of the photograph in her pack.

She had only visited Grace for a short time that summer, meeting up for a solstice festival in Glastonbury, but she remembered how the light had been so different down in Somerset.

The pace was much slower than London and people lived closer to the rhythms of the earth. Of course, that had led to one of their usual arguments when Rebecca became impatient with the lack of city conveniences, but Grace had found peace in the seasonal shifts of rural life. It would not be the verdant green of summer right now, but perhaps she might find some answers about Grace's time there. Her last known location was the village of Winbridge Hollow, which sounded idyllic, and a quiet life was exactly what she needed right now.

Rebecca emerged from the Tube at Paddington and boarded the first train heading west. As the train pulled out of the station, she glimpsed her reflection in the glass, highlighted against the backdrop of the concrete city.

She was pale and drawn, her skin sallow, her eyes sunken, with dark shadows underneath. Her titian hair, once rich and thick, was now stringy, and she was too thin, a faded negative of the vibrant woman she had been in that photograph with Grace.

As the train whizzed past the stations of outer London, Rebecca noticed a patch of colour in the tangle of hair near her temple.

A drop of paint the colour of blood.

She reached up and tried to brush it away, but no matter how hard she tried, the stain remained.

CHAPTER 3

IT WAS LATE AFTERNOON by the time Rebecca stepped off the local bus in the village of Winbridge Hollow after a connection from the train station in the city of Bath.

The village nestled in the crook of two intersecting valleys, surrounded by rolling hills and an expanse of sky that seemed to dwarf the tiny settlement. A few narrow streets of cottages surrounded a village green, and a copse of beech trees sheltered a small church with an overgrown cemetery. The sun was low in the sky, but even in the early dusk, Rebecca was struck by the stark contrast to the grey of London.

Delicate white petals of blackthorn bloomed in the hedgerows by the side of the road, highlighted by a splash of colour from wild violets and yellow celandines nestled beneath. Patches of primroses and the last of the daffodils bloomed next to a war memorial cross, its weathered stone providing shelter from the crisp wind. Moss and lichen clung to its crevices, growing out of the carved names of the long dead, evidence of life on even the darkest days.

A robin darted into the close-knit branches of the blackthorn, trilling its song. Rebecca couldn't help but smile at its optimism. There was birdsong in London, of course, but it was hard to hear with traffic at all hours of the day, unless you lived close enough to one of the parks and could be there early.

Out here, it was quiet. So quiet. She could hear everything.

The city girl in Rebecca felt a twinge of discomfort, a sudden sense of being out of place here among the untamed hedgerows and the wide, open sky with no towering buildings to break its vast canopy. It was disconcerting in a way, but there were no angry protestors, and for that, she was grateful.

Rebecca took a deep breath, noticing how even the air tasted different here. It was rich with damp earth and wild herbs, and she caught the scent of smoke in the air from a wood burner in one of the cottages.

The lights were still on in the village shop, its window filled with an assortment of local produce. Jars of preserves with handwritten labels stood next to a basket of potatoes still dusted with earth. A few apples sat alongside bunches of herbs and a few bread rolls. There were even some hand-knitted scarves and hats in soft, muted shades hung from wooden pegs, next to what looked like a row of animal skulls. Strange, but probably some local tradition.

Rebecca's stomach rumbled as she walked toward the shop. She had assumed it would be easy to find somewhere to stay and a place to eat since the apps on her phone could usually get her everything she needed at short notice. She was so used to the ease of getting anything you might need in London, but out here in the country, things were different.

She shifted her backpack on her shoulders, realising how new and out of place it looked. She had bought it a while back at an outdoor shop in the middle of London, a place where customers could pretend they were about to embark on grand adventures while most never left the comforts of the city. It seemed like a silly affectation now, a reminder of how far she was from the world she knew.

Grace had been perfectly at home in the countryside, with her easy way of striking up a conversation and her ability to find simple food and shelter with strangers. But it wasn't the city way.

Rebecca pulled her phone from her pocket to search for accommodation nearby, but the signal was weak and intermittent. A flicker of panic rose within her.

She was truly cut off from the world she knew. She'd have to sleep in the hedgerow and get the bus back to civilisation in the morning.

Rebecca couldn't help but chuckle at herself. Seriously, how bad would that be, anyway? At least she could get some food in the shop and then count the hours before she gave up on this whole thing.

She slipped her phone back into her pocket and pushed open the door to the shop. The tinkling of the bell welcomed her to the warmth inside.

The shop was piled high with tins and bottles and fresh vegetables. The smell of meaty stock and herbs filled the air from a pot warming on a little stove next to a pile of crusty bread rolls.

A middle-aged woman with a face as round and welcoming as a cottage loaf emerged from a doorway behind the counter. She wore a marigold yellow apron tied around her abundant curves, and the rosy glow of a life well-lived flushed her cheeks.

"What can I do for you, my lovely?" the woman asked with a smile, her voice rich with the melodic lilt of the West Country.

"Any chance you have some soup left?"

"Of course, it's still a bit nippy out there. You'll have to drink it here if you don't have your own bowl. I mostly make it for the local oldies who bring their own."

"That would be great, thanks."

The woman ladled out a generous portion into a rustic

pottery mug and stuck a spoon in the top. "Here you go, now."

She wrapped two rolls in a napkin and handed them to Rebecca. "Eat up. You look like you need some feeding, love." She pointed at a little stool in one corner by a stack of tinned tomatoes and sweetcorn. "Sit there and eat. I just have to finish something out back. Won't be long."

As the woman bustled out of the shop, Rebecca sat down and took a sip of the soup. She savoured the rich, meaty broth, spooning out chunks of potato and carrot and munching the fresh bread. It was good to be in the warm, especially as the sun was going down outside and the late chill would soon deepen.

As she ate, Rebecca looked around the shop. An eclectic mix of everyday necessities and curious oddities lined the shelves, and she noticed a collection of roughly carved wooden figurines nestled between jars of pickled vegetables and bags of dried herbs.

The figures were twisted and gnarled, as if struggling to escape from the wood that held them. They had a kind of unfinished beauty, reminding her of Michelangelo's sculpture *The Awakening Slave*, a figure trapped within marble, his latent power held back by a prison of stone.

On one wall, there was a cork-board with a local bus timetable pinned to it, along with a flyer about a Spring Equinox celebration and beside it, an advertisement for the local award-winning vineyard, Standing Stone Cellars.

Rebecca frowned. The name rang a bell. Could Grace have worked there? It was certainly possible as she often took casual labour jobs across the seasons.

The shop owner bustled back into the room, her cheeks flushed, her eyes sparkling.

"There we are, love. All sorted in the back." She wiped her hands on her apron and leaned against the counter, assessing Rebecca with a curious gaze.

"Tourist, are you?"

Rebecca swallowed her mouthful of soup and smiled. "How did you guess? Yes, I've come down from London. I'm… on a break from my job right now and I wanted to see some of the area."

"Ah, London. I've never been. Sounds like a terrible place."

Rebecca was taken aback. How could someone who lived just a few hours away never have visited the capital of their country? Was the woman not curious about the wider world? Rebecca felt the gulf between the city and the country grow wider as she considered how different their lives were.

She nodded. "It's not for everyone."

The woman chuckled. "I've no need to leave the county here. If you're traveling around these parts, there's lots of good walking. Then there's the farms. We've some of the finest produce in the country, we do. The soil is rich and fertile, as blessed we are. Fields of wheat and barley, orchards heavy with apples and pears when the harvest is due — if you're sticking around that long?"

"I'm… not sure, to be honest." Rebecca sensed the woman's curiosity. Perhaps that was natural in a place where few outsiders visited, but she was reticent to share her exact situation.

She pointed at the advertisement. "Can I visit the vineyard?"

The woman nodded. "Oh yes, they do tours and tastings sometimes, but usually later in the year, when the grapes are ripening." She hesitated and then nodded, as if remembering something. "They are hiring at the moment, though. They need workers to tend the vines and you know, since Brexit, it's been hard to get foreign workers. You interested?"

Rebecca considered her flat back in London, the bustling streets and the stress of the building site. The thought of returning, even in a few weeks, felt suffocating. She needed space, a chance to breathe and process everything that had happened. The idea of manual labour, of working with her hands in the open air, suddenly held a strange appeal. If it didn't suit her, well, she could always leave. There was a certain freedom in that, a sense of possibility that had been lacking in her life for far too long.

And then there was Grace. If she stayed here, in this quiet corner of Somerset, perhaps she might find people who had known her sister, who could shed light on the days leading up to her disappearance.

"You know what? I think I might be interested in a job at the vineyard," Rebecca said, surprising herself with the decision.

The woman's face lit up with a broad smile. "I'm sure they'll be happy to have you, my lovely. Now, I'm closing up, so I'll have that cup back. You staying local, like?"

Rebecca stood and carried the cup and spoon over to the counter, a flush of embarrassment creeping into her cheeks. "I don't actually have anywhere lined up. I thought I could find somewhere once I arrived."

The woman tutted, but there was no judgment in her eyes, only a warm concern. "Well, that won't do at all. Tell you what, I've got a little box room upstairs. It's nothing special, mind you, but it's clean and dry, and you're welcome to it tonight. I'm Pam, by the way."

Relief flooded Rebecca, along with gratitude at the woman's unexpected generosity. "Thank you so much. That would be amazing. I'm Rebecca."

Pam smiled. "We look out for each other round here. Now, the vineyard is picking up a new batch of workers tomorrow. I could give them a call, put in a good word for you. See if they've got room for one more?"

"That would be great. Thank you so much. For everything."

"This way, then." Pam beckoned, and Rebecca followed

her out the back and up some old wooden stairs that creaked as they walked up.

The tiny box room nestled in the attic of the cottage. There was a single bed with a worn, patchwork quilt under a window, a hand-painted chest of drawers crammed beside it with an amateur oil painting above. The sloped ceiling made it hard to stand straight.

"It's not much, but it's yours for the night." Pam turned on a lamp sitting on top of the chest of drawers and pointed to a small door hidden in the shadows. "The bathroom's through there. Shower's a bit temperamental, mind you. Not much water pressure up here."

Rebecca set her pack on the floor. "I can't thank you enough for this, Pam. Really."

Pam waved away her gratitude with a smile. "Think nothing of it, my lovely. Now, I'll give Isabelle, the vineyard owner, a call, but I know the bus will be at the cross around eight o'clock. No doubt they'll appreciate an extra pair of hands."

Rebecca nodded, already feeling a sense of purpose and excitement at the prospect of working at the vineyard. "I'll be there. Eight o'clock."

Pam turned and creaked her way back downstairs, leaving Rebecca in the tiny box room. She could feel a cold draught through the edges of the window and shivered as she laid her pack on the bed.

It was a world away from where she started the day, but as she looked out into the gloom beyond the window, Rebecca was grateful she wasn't sleeping out there under the blackthorn hedge. The darkness was thick here, deeper than she'd ever experienced in London, where she had to wear an eye mask to keep out the bright street lights from the estate. The only light she could see in the village was a single flickering candle that burned in one of the church windows, casting eerie shadows across the graveyard, with its weathered headstones half sunken into the ground.

A sudden movement caught her eye.

A shadow, darker than the rest, darted between the graves. Something misshapen. Something horned.

Rebecca stepped back from the window and pulled the curtain quickly across, unsettled by whatever it was, and now even more grateful she was not outside in the dark. Grace would have laughed at her city girl imagination, and the thought made Rebecca even more determined to learn about the area.

She got ready for bed and slipped under the covers, pulling the quilt tight around her. The bedclothes smelled musty, but she was warm and dry and safe — and grateful.

As she reached over to turn off the lamp, Rebecca looked more closely at the oil painting behind it.

A circle of weathered standing stones stood amongst a wild vineyard, with tendrils from the vines reaching out to strangle the base of the stones. The style was crude, but the picture was unsettling, and was that a horned shadow in the painting's corner?

Rebecca shook her head and turned out the light. Her imagination was seriously running wild out here in the sticks. She would see everything in a new light tomorrow.

Rebecca woke with a start, her heart racing and her skin slick with sweat. The room was pitch black, and for a moment, she couldn't remember where she was. She reached out a hand to anchor herself to the wall, touching the rough stone as she remembered the events of yesterday.

Strange sounds filtered in through the draughty window frame. That must be what had woken her.

At first, she thought it might be the wind, whistling

through the cracks and crevices of the old building. But as she listened more closely, she realised it was something else entirely.

A shrill cry, followed by a series of yips and barks. Foxes maybe? There were urban foxes in London, often seen raiding bins in the early mornings, but Rebecca had never heard cries like this.

An owl hooted somewhere in the distance, and Rebecca imagined its sharp beak tearing into the flesh of some tiny rodent, devouring its steaming entrails.

She realised the countryside was not quiet at all. The night was full of sounds — the rustle of creatures in the undergrowth at the edges of the graveyard, the creak of branches in the wind, the call of night birds. If these noises existed in the city, they were masked by the ever-present traffic.

Rebecca tossed and turned, trying to block out the unsettling sounds and sink back into the oblivion of sleep. But every time she closed her eyes, the image of the horned shadow from the painting next to the bed danced behind her eyelids.

Eventually, she got up and took it off the wall and put it into a drawer. It was ridiculous, but it helped.

Rebecca eventually drifted off into fitful sleep, where she walked amongst ancient standing stones. The scent of something rotting rose from the pungent vegetation as a thick mist curled around her feet. At the edge of her vision, a horned shadow flitted between the stones, its dark gaze both an invitation and a challenge.

CHAPTER 4

THE NEXT MORNING, REBECCA repacked her bag and placed the oil painting back on the wall, although something about it must be crooked as she couldn't seem to hang it quite straight. Hopefully Pam wouldn't notice.

She made her way down the creaky stairs as the scent of fresh bread and strong coffee wafted up from the kitchen below. Pam was already bustling about, her apron dusted with flour as she pulled a tray of steaming cheese scones from the oven.

"Morning, my lovely. I hope you slept well."

Rebecca nodded. "Yes, thank you, what a cosy room, and so quiet compared to my place in London."

Pam handed her a warm scone wrapped in a paper towel and pointed at a mug of freshly made coffee. "Eat that quickly now. The bus will be here soon."

"Thanks, I really appreciate your help."

Rebecca gratefully tucked in. When she checked her phone, she had one bar of service, so she sent a message to Alan, her manager, explaining she was taking an extended leave of absence and would be in touch once she was ready to come back.

A few minutes later, she headed out the door of the shop into the crisp morning air.

The village was cloaked in a hazy mist that clung to the hedgerows and softened the edges of the cottages. Four people stood near the war memorial cross, slightly apart from each other as they waited for the minibus that would take them to the vineyard. Rebecca walked over to join them.

An older woman with short, grey hair and bright, bird-like eyes crouched down by a crack in the memorial's base, her fingers gently tracing the petals of a tiny, yellow flower that sprouted there. She murmured something under her breath, pulled out a small notebook tucked into her pocket, and scribbled notes with a half-chewed Biro.

Nearby, an elegant young woman with long, black hair and high cheekbones leaned against a low wall, inspecting her immaculate nails. She wore a tailored designer jacket more suited to a London office than a day in the fields, and Rebecca was pleased to see that she carried a bag even newer than her own.

A few metres away, clearly keeping his distance, a wiry, middle-aged man with a shock of black hair stood slightly hunched, as very tall men often do. His face was etched with deeper lines than was normal in a man his age, and his eyes held a distant, haunted look. He wore an olive wood cross around his neck.

The last figure turned to look at Rebecca as she approached, his gaze direct and assessing. The man had the solid, well-built frame of someone accustomed to physical labour, with broad shoulders and strong, capable hands. His sandy blonde hair was cropped short, practical and unfussy, and the faint lines around his eyes spoke of long hours outdoors.

"Morning, I'm Ben," he said as Rebecca reached the group, holding out a hand.

His accent was distinct, the rich, lilting cadence of the northeast a stark contrast to the local dialect. Another outsider of a kind. She couldn't help but notice the way his jacket stretched across his chest, straining slightly against the taut muscles beneath. His hand, when she shook it, was calloused and rough. Clearly a man used to physical labour.

"I'm Rebecca. Are you waiting for the bus to the vineyard?"

Ben nodded. "Yes, it should be here soon. I'm here as a replacement maintenance engineer, and also helping in the vines. How about you?"

Rebecca didn't know how to describe her escape from eco-protestors and a doxxing on social media. It's possible that her actions would be frowned upon by locals anyway, and she certainly didn't want to mention her missing sister at this stage.

She shrugged. "I just needed a break from the city. I'm not even sure I'm going to stay."

The elegant young woman stepped away from the wall. "I'm Asha, and I am definitely not here for manual labour. I'm in marketing."

Of course you are, Rebecca thought, while outwardly smiling without judgment.

The older woman stood up, put her notebook away, and brushed dirt from her hands. "I'm Helen, and this lovely little flower here is a Ranunculus ficaria, commonly known as the lesser celandine. It's one of the first to bloom in spring. I'm hoping to learn more about the biodynamic practices used at the vineyard. They can be strange but also most effective."

Ben turned to the tall man. "And what about you, mate? What's your name?"

The dark-haired man was silent a moment before he spoke with a terse reply. "Liam."

Ben raised an eyebrow at the rest of the group. "Okay, then. I guess we'll be getting to know each other later."

The roar of an engine came from out of the mist and a rickety old school bus headed their way. It was painted green, converted from its better days carrying rural schoolchildren into a means to transport tourists and workers to the vineyard.

Its brakes squealed as it pulled up beside the war memorial.

The driver's door swung open, and a woman stepped out, her presence commanding immediate attention.

"Good morning, everyone! I'm Isabelle Holt, owner of Standing Stone Cellars and vineyard."

With her silver hair cropped short and muscular figure, Isabelle was a handsome woman in her early sixties and she exuded an energetic vitality. Her accent was a curious mix of British landed upper class and rural Somerset. She had a designer silk scarf tied around her neck, its vibrant colours a stark contrast to the soil-stained green dungarees she wore.

"Looks like we're all here. Now, let's not dally. We've a full day ahead."

Pam bustled out of the village shop with a cardboard box laden with baked goods. Isabelle went to help her. "Thanks, these smell amazing."

Isabelle loaded up the box into the back, while Rebecca and the others boarded the bus, settling into the worn but comfortable seats.

As they left the village behind, the landscape opened up before them in a patchwork of fields and rolling hills, with great expanses of spring green.

Soon, the narrow, winding roads were flanked by high hedgerows and towering trees, their branches stretching overhead, forming a cage across the sky. The weak spring sun tried to pierce the dark clouds, but the grey was too strong, suffocating the rays until they faded into gloom.

They passed a turnoff. "Down there, that's Mabel's farm. She supplies the most marvellous eggs and chicken manure for our compost." Isabelle pointed to wide fields on the left. "And that's old Tom's land and woods beyond. He brings us venison."

Rebecca soon lost track of all the names of the locals and their children and the new animals born and the various disasters that seemed to befall them as Isabelle continued her monologue.

There was clearly an intricate web of connection bonding the community here, where so many lived and died within the same area. Their ancestors were buried under the same stones. Their decomposing flesh fed the rich soil that, in turn, produced a harvest to feed the next generation. It was a far cry from the anonymity of London, where even neighbours remained strangers. Life was more than work here, and the land mattered. Had Grace found at least a temporary home here?

As they twisted and turned along the narrow lanes, Rebecca felt a sense of disorientation wash over her. The high hedgerows obscured any landmarks or points of reference, making it impossible to gauge their direction or distance. It was as if they had been swallowed up by the countryside, lost in a labyrinth that only locals could find their way out of.

As an architect, Rebecca appreciated how these ancient borders had been planted to delineate farms, using natural materials to form the barriers. Much later, roads were built to wind between them, but even now they seemed out of place. It was slightly terrifying to watch Isabelle drive so fast along the narrow lanes, with hedgerows so thick and high on either side that any oncoming traffic meant both vehicles had to stop, and one party reverse until they found a passing place, only slightly wider than the rest of the lane.

Rebecca pulled out her phone to check where they were on the maps app, only to see the last signal bar dwindle to nothing until it disappeared entirely.

A momentary panic gripped her, fingers tightening around the device that normally tethered her to what she considered real about her world. How did she know where she was without it?

CHAPTER 5

REBECCA TOOK A DEEP breath to calm herself and gazed back out at the hedgerows. She needed time away from London, and she didn't want to see the hate fired at her on social media. A few weeks away from her phone and civilisation would do her good, and then she could hitch a ride back to the city when she was ready. She tried to relax as the bus took them deeper into the countryside.

They wound through a final stretch of narrow lanes on top of a hill, and the hedgerows suddenly gave way to reveal a breathtaking vista. The vineyard sat in a natural amphitheatre, its south-facing slopes capturing every precious ray of English sunshine. The rows of vines followed the contours of the land, cascading down gentle slopes towards a line of ancient oak trees that marked the edge of cultivated land before it met wild forest. There was also a sprawling mansion house, behind which lay a curious high fence made of ancient pointed staves, perhaps protecting the land beyond.

On one incline, a labyrinth of vines spiralled across the hill — a curious design for a vineyard planting, but it seemed so right for this setting. From this vantage point, it almost resembled a whirlpool, drawing the eye inexorably towards its centre. Rebecca blinked, suddenly dizzy, and forced herself to look away.

"Almost there!" Isabelle announced with enthusiasm.

They passed the sign to the vineyard entrance nailed to an old, gnarled oak, its branches twisting toward the heavens. As they drove past, Rebecca noticed something hanging from one particularly tormented limb.

A tiny horned animal skull.

A flash of her nightmare made Rebecca gasp, and she turned it into a cough to hide her reaction.

"You alright?" Ben asked.

Rebecca nodded and smiled. "Yes, just desperate to get out of this bus."

Isabelle drove on deeper into the property, skirting the rows of vines. Their twisted trunks spoke of age and resilience, each knot a record of seasons past. The canes stretched upward, awaiting the warmth that would eventually coax the tiny tender buds into clusters of ripening fruit.

Isabelle wound down her window and thrust her arm out, gesturing over her land. "Commercial vineyards keep their alleys sterile, the easier to drive machines through, but we encourage biodiversity here. The more species of plant we have, the better the soil, the better the crop and the taste of the wine. You can see grasses coming up already and some celandines amongst the yarrow and clover. We'll have ox-eye daisies and wildflowers blooming soon."

The air blowing in the window was alive with the promise of abundance. The rich, loamy scent of earth mingled with the sharp, green fragrance of fresh growth, and a faint, mineral tang as if from a water source, maybe a nearby stream.

High above, a buzzard circled, its broad wings cutting through the air with an eerie grace as it wove a hypnotic dance, each turn slow and deliberate as it scanned the patchwork of land for prey.

As they passed by the vines, Rebecca noticed curious carvings on the end-posts, not numbered markers as she expected, but lines cut into primitive figures and symbols. Some were human-like or floral, others more bestial. Helen had said the vineyard used biodynamic practices, and although Rebecca didn't know what that meant exactly, it might explain the strange elements. Or maybe it was just the countryside, and she was a city girl out of her depth.

Isabelle pulled up near a cluster of buildings that blended seamlessly into the landscape. The winery was housed in a converted seventeenth-century barn, its honey-coloured stone glowing warmly even in the chill spring sunlight. Nearby, a modern structure of glass and timber served as the tasting room, its large windows reflecting the vineyard and the sky.

"Welcome to Standing Stone Cellars," Isabelle announced with a note of pride. "There have been vines here since Roman times, perhaps even before. The terroir here is quite special, you see. The soil is rich in minerals, and the micro-climate created by those hills" — she gestured towards the distant rise — "is perfect for growing grapes."

As Isabelle spoke, a figure emerged from between the rows of vines, striding purposefully towards the group. A stocky man, broad-shouldered and weather-beaten, with a face that spoke of years working this land. A full beard partially hid a scar on one cheekbone, and his eyes were a startling shade of green, almost reptilian, seeming to take in everything at once.

"Ah, here's Nate." Isabelle turned to greet him. "Everyone, this is Nate Marshall, our vineyard manager. Nate, these are our new recruits."

Nate nodded in greeting, his gaze sweeping over them all. When his eyes met Rebecca's, she felt a jolt of… something. Recognition? Curiosity? She couldn't quite place it.

"Morning, all," Nate said, his voice deep and gravelly. "I hope you're ready for some hard work."

Ben stepped forward, extending his hand. "Looking forward to it. I'm Ben, the new maintenance engineer."

Nate shook his hand firmly. "Good to have you on board, Ben. We've got quite a few things that need fixing."

Helen piped up next, her eyes bright with enthusiasm. "I'm Helen, and I'm particularly interested in your biodynamic practices. Do you follow the lunar calendar for your vineyard operations?"

A smile tugged at the corner of Nate's mouth. "That we do. Been following Steiner's methods for years now. Makes a difference, though some folks think we're barmy. But you'll certainly learn more about that."

Asha cleared her throat delicately. "I'm Asha. I'll be working on marketing strategies for the vineyard."

Nate nodded acknowledgment, then turned his attention to Liam, who stood slightly apart from the group. "And you are?"

"Liam. Here for whatever you need."

Nate turned to Rebecca. "And that leaves you. What's your story? I hear you decided to come on short notice?"

Rebecca hesitated, acutely aware of the curious glances from the others. "I'm Rebecca. I'm on leave from my architectural company and, well, I'm here to help out with anything, I guess."

Nate held her gaze for a moment longer than necessary, and Rebecca had the uncomfortable feeling that he saw more than she intended to reveal. But he simply nodded and turned back to the group.

"Right then. Leave your bags. We'll start with a tour of the vineyard. You'll need to know your way around if you're going to be of any use."

Nate led the group away from the bus, his weathered boots crunching on the gravel path. "Right then, let's start with the basics. As Helen said, here at Standing Stone, we follow biodynamic practices. It's not just about avoiding chemicals, mind you. It's about treating the whole vineyard as a living organism, and allowing the land to flourish by restoring its energy through the balance of elements."

He paused near a row of vines, running his calloused hand along a gnarly trunk. "These vines, they're not just plants. They're conduits between earth and sky, transforming sunlight and soil into something... transcendent. After all, what is wine but a way that humans have always used to rise above the brutality of daily life?"

They approached a small, unassuming shed near the edge of the vineyard. Nate unlocked the heavy wooden door and the group filed in. Rebecca blinked as her eyes adjusted to the dim interior.

The preparation shed was a curious blend of farmhouse practicality and esoteric mysticism. Bundles of herbs hung from the rafters, their pungent aroma mingling with the earthier scent of soil and compost. Rows of glass jars filled with different liquids stood on wooden shelves, some tinged with colour from flowers and herbs, some containing what looked like bones.

Nate gestured to a corner where a cattle horn sat on a workbench. "These are one of our most important tools. We fill them with a special preparation and bury them over winter. Come spring, it's transformed into a powerful fertiliser that we use on the vines. If you stay, you will learn more about these practices."

Nate clearly noticed the look on their faces. "You may have your doubts, but the results are worth it. You will see the many awards the vineyard has won in the tasting room later."

As they walked out, Rebecca looked back at the strange shed. There was something about the place that felt charged, as if the air hummed with unseen energies she couldn't understand, something lost in the city where people lived so disconnected from the earth.

They continued their walk through the vineyard, as Nate pointed out different blocks of grape varieties.

"We use Pinot Noir in our red and sparkling wines. It

thrives in cooler climates, so it's perfect for Somerset. The block at the top is Bacchus, a white, and this is Solaris, also white, which ripens earlier."

As the group trailed after him, Rebecca noticed more curious carvings peering out from fence posts, trellises, and even the bark of trees. This figure she recognized from one of her art history courses — it was the face of the Green Man, leafy and wild, an ancient symbol of nature and rebirth used in pagan celebration but also carved within the Gothic cathedrals of England.

Embedded in the gnarled trunk of an ancient oak on the edge of the vine rows, one particular face emerged with disturbing realism.

The lines of his face were not the gentle, flowing curves of traditional carving but jagged and cruel, each leaf a serrated knife. His expression was one of almost malevolent glee, a twisted smile that spoke of ancient curses and forgotten rites. Vine leaves slithered around the corners of his eyes, creeping tendrils that hinted at the possibility of movement when no one was watching. The dark, carved pits of his eyes followed her as she passed and Rebecca shivered, pulling her jacket tighter despite the warming day.

CHAPTER 6

NATE LED THE GROUP on, and they rounded a corner to find an older man bent over a wheelbarrow full of rich, dark compost, as he spaded it out and worked it into the soil between rows of vines.

"That's our special compost blend," Nate explained. "We add different kinds of organic matter to enrich the soil. Herbs, minerals, even animal organs and blood. It's all part of the biodynamic process."

The man's spade bit into the earth as he turned over the dark soil. A glint of white caught Rebecca's eye, and she squinted, trying to make out what it was.

"Are those bones?" she asked, her voice barely above a whisper.

Nate nodded, unperturbed. "All return to the earth, eventually... Some sooner than others."

As they continued their tour, the group crested a gentle hill, revealing a new vista of the vineyard. In a fenced area between vine rows, a small flock of sheep grazed contentedly, their woolly bodies stark against the rich earth as they moved methodically through the rows.

"Our four-legged workers," Nate explained. "They keep the weeds down and fertilise as they go. Nature's perfect lawn mowers, they are." He pointed to the lower fields. "We have beehives, and chickens who eat the pests, scratch up weeds, and fertilise the soil as well. We are almost entirely a closed system here."

"Why is that so important?" Helen asked as she scribbled in her notebook.

Nate took a deep breath, filling his lungs with the air of the vineyard. "You can smell the earth here. It's alive, and that's what we seek to retain in the wine. What we call 'terroir' is essentially a combination of climate, soil, topography, microclimate, and the human and animal aspects of everything that goes into a wine. Biodynamics seeks to maximise the terroir, so every single drop of wine made here at Standing Stone is a distillation of the land, an expression of the unique ecosystem that you are now a part of."

Nate gestured to the landscape before them. "Why would you want it any other way?"

Helen sighed happily, her face almost transfigured as she looked out over the landscape. Nate certainly had one convert to the biodynamic cause, but Rebecca couldn't help her urban cynicism.

She pushed it down as she scanned the vineyard, trying to see more than just the beauty of the land. It was a living ecosystem that nurtured grapes that made the wine, that brought success to the vineyard and the surrounding community. And they certainly had success. Standing Stone Cellars had won many of the major wine awards, so who was she to judge their unusual practices?

Rebecca noticed the high fence of pointed staves at the edge of an ancient wooded section, but the lay of the land meant whatever was directly behind it was hidden. "Is that area part of the vineyard's terroir?" she asked, pointing it out.

Nate paused a moment. "We leave some of the most ancient land for the wild grapes to grow as they like, for nature to do its own thing with none of our control or influence. That section of the vineyard is strictly off-limits, except on special festivals when the community gathers by the standing stones for which we are named. The wild grapes are used to make our most exclusive wine."

Asha gasped. "Seriously? The Horned God's Share. Wow! That wine is so rare. I'd love to make some social content in that section. Are you sure it's off-limits?"

"Definitely." Nate's tone was curt and his eyes steel-hard. "I'll show you the gates so you know exactly what to avoid, but anyone found there will be escorted off site immediately."

"Okay, okay." Asha raised her hands in surrender. "Do we at least get to taste the wine?"

Nate shrugged. "That depends on so many things."

He walked away down the hill. "I'll show you the staff quarters next."

Ben hurried after him, asking detailed questions about the vineyard's operations, while Rebecca and the others followed more slowly.

Asha took lots of photos, arty shots of the vines and a few selfies. Helen scribbled furiously in her notebook, utterly absorbed as she occasionally bent to examine a plant as they passed. Liam's face was a mask, his gaze fixed into the distance, remaining aloof.

They were an odd bunch, for sure, but then this was an odd vineyard with its carvings and biodynamic practices and wild, untamed, off-limit places. Rebecca could see Grace fitting in here, with her deep knowledge of nature and the seasons and her acceptance of the unusual. But her sister was also not one to obey the rules of men. Would she have trespassed into the restricted area?

At the bottom of the hill, Nate led the group back through the cluster of buildings and into a cavernous space filled with concrete tanks, where the yeasty aroma of past fermentations gave a sense of the transformation within.

"This is where we take what the land gives us and turn it

into wine." His voice echoed slightly in the large room. "Each tank is carefully monitored to ensure optimal fermentation conditions."

They passed through a heavy wooden door into the barrel room.

The change in atmosphere was immediate. Rows upon rows of barrels stretched into the shadows, each bearing the distinctive logo of Standing Stone Cellars, and the cool, damp air was redolent with the rich aroma of oak and ageing wine.

As Rebecca's eyes adjusted to the dim light, she noticed something curious. Many of the barrels bore strange symbols painted in what looked like red ochre. They weren't uniform; each barrel had its own unique markings.

"They're vintage markers," Nate said, following her gaze. "We use a lunar calendar to determine the optimal times for various vineyard activities. Each symbol represents a unique combination of celestial influences present during that particular vintage."

He ran his hand over one barrel, tracing a symbol that looked like a crescent moon intersected by three wavy lines. "This one, for instance, represents a harvest done during the waning moon in Pisces. Makes for a wine with particular depth."

Rebecca nodded as she examined some of the barrels more closely, the symbols drawing her in. It was strange to think that every single barrel would be different, that there was no methodological way to ensure they tasted the same. Each would be an original expression of the terroir and the mix of grapes and the seasons of that particular year. She had never thought about wine so deeply before, merely drank it with pleasure.

She bent down to examine a particular barrel with markings that looked different to the others, the symbol more like a distorted face, but with too many eyes. Its mouth gaped open in a silent scream and Rebecca stood up quickly, unable to tear her gaze from its disturbing features.

CHAPTER 7

"Let's move along now." Nate's sharp tone interrupted Rebecca's thoughts, and she turned to see him looking at her in particular.

They continued through to the bottling line, with its symphony of whirring machines and clinking glass. "We time our bottling with the rhythms of the earth," Nate explained. "The moon's gravitational pull affects more than just the tides, you know."

He led them on towards a row of wooden racks, their angled frames cradling dozens of bottles, necks down. "These are riddling racks, essential in our traditional method of sparkling wine production. The bottles were filled last winter, and have been aging on the lees ever since, building character."

Nate took hold of the base of a bottle and gave it a precise, measured turn. "This helps the sediment settle, and in the final process, we disgorge the residue, add a final touch of sweetness, and seal them up again." He lightly tapped the riddling rack. "Be careful in here though. These bottles are under intense pressure, and we wouldn't want anyone to get hurt."

Nate led them out and into reached a more conventional-looking business area with desks, computers, and filing cabinets, topped with piles of rolled labels. "This is where the less romantic but equally important work happens," Nate said, chuckling. "Labelling, marketing, shipping, logistics, financials. All the things that turn our wine from a beautiful secret into a product people can actually enjoy."

He turned to Asha. "This is where you'll be spending most of your time."

Asha nodded. "I look forward to getting started, and I presume you have better internet access here? I can't get any signal on my phone."

Nate nodded. "Of course. Isabelle will show you everything later."

As the others followed Nate out, Rebecca lingered by a desk that must belong to Isabelle. Peeking out from a stack of papers was the corner of a book, its leather cover cracked and mottled with age. Perhaps the book might give some clue to the ancient practices of the vineyard?

She glanced out the door.

The others were only metres away, asking Nate questions about the business practices of the vineyard. But none of them were looking in her direction.

She reached out, her fingers trembling slightly as she gently lifted the papers away and touched the book.

Its cover was a deep, oxblood red, the colour of wine left too long in the glass. The leather was tooled with intricate patterns, organic shapes and runes that seemed to shift and change when she wasn't looking directly at them. The embossed title was still visible in faded gold: *Viticulture and the Old Ways: A Grimoire*.

Her heart pounding with a sense of trespass, Rebecca carefully opened the book, wincing at the crackle of the ancient spine. The pages within were thick parchment covered in dense text written in a spidery hand, interspersed with illustrations that bordered on the macabre.

One page showed winemaking at different phases of the

moon, each illustration surrounded by gnarled vines, twisting and writhing across the page. Their leaves were sharp, as if edged with blades, while the presses dripped with a liquid too dark and thick to be mere grape juice.

"Rebecca?"

Nate's voice made her jump. She closed the book and quickly rearranged the papers before hurrying outside, smiling as she rejoined the group. "I was just looking at the beautiful calligraphy on the labels. What's next?"

Nate's gaze lingered on hers before he turned to lead them on further into the clutch of buildings until they emerged by the wall of ancient staves. The wood was stained almost black, and thick ropes of ivy wound their way up and around the posts. There was a double gate that would open up to a wide entrance, but it was barred with a heavy carved log marked by a carved slash of lines interwoven with what looked like horns.

"This is as far as you go."

He placed a hand on the gate, and his voice changed to a more reverent tone. "This is the heart of Standing Stone. It is the oldest part of the vineyard, dating back to Roman times almost two thousand years ago and nurtured ever since by those in the community who love this land. You may come inside with the community at Samhain."

Nate turned away, muttering under his breath. Rebecca, standing closest to him, caught his words. "If you make it that far."

She couldn't blame his doubt at their suitability. She didn't even know if she'd make it to next week. But his words struck a stubborn chord within her, fed by curiosity at the strange things she had seen already. Perhaps this could be a new start, a place to learn a completely different organic style she could bring back to the city after a break. It would certainly help her stand out, and she could feel ideas beginning to emerge already.

As the group walked away from the fenced section, Rebecca glanced through a gap in the staves. She glimpsed a tangle of ancient vines and a flash of something large and dark, something horned, darting between them. She blinked, and it was gone.

"Now for the part you've all been waiting for," Nate said. "The tasting room, where you'll try some of our wines. The work starts tomorrow, but for today, it's time to taste the terroir."

The tasting room was an elegant, high-ceilinged space with exposed wooden beams and large windows with sweeping views of the vines outside. Several brass spittoons stood discreetly on polished wooden tables, their wide, flared rims designed to catch the swirl and splash of discarded wine, preserving the palate for the next nuanced pour.

The walls were adorned with vintage photographs depicting the vineyard's long history, and Rebecca noticed a photo of a younger Isabelle standing next to a man, their arms wrapped around each other, clearly in love, with a little girl standing in front of them holding a rustic corn dolly in her hands.

Nate gestured for everyone to take a seat at the polished wooden tables as kitchen workers came in with platters of local meats and cheese, bread, and crackers.

"Right then, let's get to the best part of the job, shall we?" Nate pulled an array of bottles from a nearby rack and Asha helped to hand out the first set of glasses. "Sparkling rosé first."

As he poured, the rich aroma of wine filled the air and they soon relaxed in each other's company. Nate shared stories about each vintage, his passion evident in every word.

As Rebecca savoured each mouthful, she wondered why she had even felt there was anything strange here. This was a magical place where they transformed vines and soil and sun into something that brought people pleasure. It was such a long way from the violence of the protests in London, and from people who hated her for destroying nature. Here, she could be part of nurturing the land, using her hands and her energy to grow something wonderful. She might even emerge renewed.

Ben leaned in close, his voice low, and she caught a scent of pine forests from his skin. "What do you think of the place, then? Think you might stay awhile?"

There was an invitation in his eyes, and Rebecca sensed the warmth between them wasn't entirely because of the wine.

She smiled. "Yes, I think I have a lot to learn here."

The group relaxed, and the wine flowed as they tried more vintages while the sun went down over the vineyard.

Rebecca enjoyed the buzz of the wine, and the exquisite selection of local produce. It was as if everything tasted real here, not like the plastic-wrapped supermarket food she was used to. She tried to buy organic and grass-fed when she could, but this produce was truly local and perhaps she could already taste the terroir.

Ben's hand brushed against hers as he reached for his glass, and his gaze lingered a moment longer than necessary. Perhaps there would be even more for her here than just working the land.

Isabelle swept into the room, her presence immediately commanding attention. "Welcome again, all of you. I hope Nate hasn't bored you too much with his talk of cosmic energies and lunar cycles."

Nate feigned offence, prompting laughter from the group, and she waved his comments aside with a grin.

"Time to show you the bunk rooms and turn in before you drink all the profits. It will be an early start tomorrow. There's a lot to learn and much to be done."

She looked pointedly at Nate.

"Alright, alright. Fun's over." He winked. "For tonight at least."

The group made their way to the bunkhouses with an easy camaraderie; the jokes continuing as their breath misted in the chill of the night. Even Liam seemed more relaxed, although he had remained quiet while others shared stories of their lives.

"Men's bunks in there," Nate said, pointing. "Women's over here. Shared bathrooms over there. Breakfast at seven. Night all."

He spun away, leaving the group to separate. Ben and Liam went into the men's accommodation, and Rebecca, Helen, and Asha into the women's.

The inside was lit by a single, dim bulb hanging from the ceiling, casting a soft, golden glow over the room. Rough-hewn oak planks lined the walls, and the floor creaked underfoot with each step.

There were ranks of sturdy bunk beds, their frames made of the same dark oak, each one with simple sheets and duvets. Woollen blankets, in muted natural shades, were folded at the foot of each bed. A small, pot-bellied stove sat in one corner, radiating a comforting warmth that took the edge off the night's chill.

There were already a few people in bed, asleep—other temporary workers perhaps, exhausted by the day's work—so the newcomers remained quiet.

Rebecca claimed the lower bunk closest to one of the windows as the others settled into their beds. She could still taste the evening's wine on her tongue, a lingering sweetness mixed with the crisp night air.

As she pulled the blanket around her, Rebecca opened the curtain a little and gazed out of the window. The vineyard stretched before her, bathed in silvery moonlight. There were no clouds, and the stars were bright overhead.

She thought of her flat in London, the view of human-constructed concrete and brick she'd grown so accustomed to. How different it would be to wake up in this place every morning, to breathe in the clean country air, to feel connected to the rhythms of the land. Perhaps, if she stayed long enough, she would feel closer to Grace, and understand why her sister shunned the city and those who loved the urban life.

The harsh clanging of a bell shattered the stillness of the night, jolting Rebecca from a deep sleep. For a moment, she was utterly disoriented, struggling to make sense of the unfamiliar surroundings and the insistent ringing that seemed to reverberate through her bones.

Darkness pressed in from all sides, broken only by slivers of moonlight sneaking through the gaps in the curtains. Rebecca fumbled for her phone, squinting at the too-bright screen. 2:17 a.m. Her head throbbed, a reminder of the wine they'd shared just hours before.

Before she could fully process what was happening, Nate's voice boomed through the bunkhouse, urgent and commanding.

"Get up! It's an emergency! Get dressed quickly!"

CHAPTER 8

AROUND HER, REBECCA COULD hear the rustle of blankets and confused mumbling as the other women stirred. Asha's voice cut through the darkness, sharp with irritation. "What the hell is going on?"

Rebecca swung her legs out of bed, wincing as her bare feet touched the cold wooden floor. She groped in the darkness for her clothes, her fingers clumsy with sleep and residual alcohol. She pulled on a pair of jeans and a jacket over her T-shirt, shoving her feet into her boots.

As she stumbled out of the bunkhouse, the chill hit her like a physical blow. Her breath frosted in the air, and she hugged herself tightly as her head cleared in the cold. The night was still, with the kind of crystalline beauty that heralded dangerously low temperatures.

In the pale moonlight, Rebecca could see figures moving among the vines. Isabelle's voice carried through the darkness, issuing rapid-fire instructions. Other workers were already spreading out across the vineyard.

Nate appeared at her elbow, startling her. "It's a frost. Come on," he said, his voice gruff with urgency. "We need to get the bougies out. Follow me."

"Bougies?" Rebecca asked as she stumbled after him.

He led her to a storage shed with stacks of oversized candles in metal pots.

"Frost candles, made from our own beeswax," Nate explained as he piled them into her arms along with a lighter. "They help keep the air temperature up just enough to save the new buds on the vines. We have to get them placed and lit as fast as possible or we could lose the entire year's crop."

Rebecca followed Nate back out into the vineyard, the frost crunching under her feet as they walked. The vines, poised to burst with new life, now seemed fragile and vulnerable in the biting cold.

"Space them out," Isabelle called, her breath visible in the frigid air. "One every few metres. Hurry now!"

Rebecca moved down the rows, setting out the candles as instructed. Her fingers, numb with cold, fumbled with the lighter, but soon the wicks caught, and the candles began to burn. She saw Ben a few rows over, his face set in concentration as he worked, and nearby, Asha wrestled with a particularly stubborn wick.

There was an urgency about the team as they worked together to try and help the land. If one severe frost could wipe out the new bud growth, the success of this vintage hung in the balance.

Slowly, pinpricks of light appeared throughout the vineyard as more and more candles were lit. The flames danced in the chill air, casting flickering shadows across the frosted ground as hundreds of tiny fires held back the killing cold, a stark contrast to the silver sheen of frost that blanketed the ground.

The candles created a boundary between earth and sky, a constellation that mirrored the stars above. It was as if they warded off more than just frost, but perhaps the encroaching void of night itself. The waxy perfume from the candles rose with the heat, swirling amongst the buds on the vines.

Rebecca stopped to catch her breath. The vineyard had been transformed into an otherworldly place, a blend of frost and firelight in the mist, an almost liminal space that seemed out of time. She could imagine people walking here back in Roman times, two thousand years ago, using the same handmade wax candles to drive the frost away from new vines, and a community stretching back generations, protecting this beautiful place.

"Keep moving!" Nate's voice broke through her reverie. "We're not done yet!"

Rebecca shook off her fatigue and grabbed another crate of candles, noticing Nate heading off towards the restricted area of ancient staves with a stack of candles in his arms. He ducked around the side, furthest from the gate, and must have used a hidden entrance, as moments later, a flicker of light came through the gaps in the wood as he looked after the wild vines, too.

The hours passed in a blur of icy fingers, flickering flames, and the scent of burning wax.

As the eastern sky began to lighten, the frantic activity gave way to a sense of quiet anticipation. Nate and Isabelle walked around the vines, checking on the buds, and the workers stood waiting to see if their efforts had paid off.

Eventually, Isabelle returned, a wide smile on her face. "The temperature's rising. Thank you all for your efforts."

Rebecca couldn't help but smile, a sense of euphoria blossoming within at being part of something so elemental.

Helen reached out and hugged her. "We did it! How exciting!"

The older woman's enthusiasm was infectious and Ben met Rebecca's grin with one of his own.

Isabelle called across the crowd, "Time to warm up with an early breakfast."

She led them all to the simple dining hall and kitchens, out the back of the main buildings. Steam rose invitingly from a large urn, and the rich aroma of hot chocolate and coffee filled the air. Plates of freshly baked pastries lay piled high next to muesli bars and fruit.

Rebecca grabbed a coffee and wrapped her numb hands around the warm mug, savouring the heat that seeped into her palms and the taste of the bitter black.

As the new workers stood there, sipping their drinks and stamping their feet to keep warm, a sense of camaraderie settled over the group. They had faced the first challenge together and made it through. Asha looked so much younger with no makeup, and her previously perfect hair in disarray, while Helen bustled about making new friends. Ben had smudges of candle soot on his cheeks, which only highlighted his cheekbones, and even the taciturn Liam seemed more relaxed. They all exchanged tired smiles, a wordless acknowledgment of their shared experience.

Rebecca thought again of Grace and wondered whether she had ever experienced a night like this. Had she stood and watched the dawn break over the frost-candled vines? It had been a magical night for sure, something she had never thought to experience. There were so many more things she wanted to learn about, and it made Rebecca more determined to stay.

A few hours later, showered and changed, Rebecca made her way to the vineyard's main building. As she approached, she saw Nate conferring with a group of workers, his weathered face serious as he gestured towards sections of the vineyard, sending them off in different directions.

"Ah, Rebecca," Nate called out as he noticed her. "Good, you're here. You'll be working with Branwen today. She's one of our most experienced workers and will show you the ropes."

He nodded towards an elderly woman standing slightly apart from the group, as gnarled and twisted as the vines themselves, her face a maze of deep wrinkles that spoke of a lifetime working outdoors. Despite her age, Branwen walked tall, and her brown eyes were curious and startlingly bright in her weathered face as she assessed Rebecca.

"Come, we have much work to do."

Without waiting for a response, Branwen turned and made her way down the rows of vines, her gait surprisingly spry. Rebecca hurried to keep up, nearly tripping over the uneven ground.

"Watch your step," Branwen called back over her shoulder. "The earth here has a mind of its own, and will take your suffering if you give it."

They stopped at a section of vines that looked, to Rebecca's untrained eye, exactly like all the others. Branwen handed her a pair of pruning shears, the metal cool and heavy in Rebecca's hands.

"Now, watch closely." With movements that belied her age, Branwen pruned the vine. Her gnarled hands moved with a fluid grace, snipping here and there with precision. "You see? Gentle but firm. The vine knows what it wants to be. We just help it along and focus its energy on where the grapes will grow."

Rebecca nodded, trying to absorb the intricacies of which cane would be chosen, and which would be culled for the good of the vine. When it was her turn, however, she found the task far more challenging than Branwen made it appear. Her cuts were clumsy, either too shallow or too deep, and more than once she nearly snipped her own fingers.

"Like this." Branwen gently corrected Rebecca's grip on the shears. "Look at the vine first, see how it's growing, then touch it. Really feel it beneath your skin. In this way, it will tell you where to cut. You just have to listen."

As they worked their way down the row, Rebecca gradually found a rhythm. The repetitive motion was almost meditative, and time seemed to pass more quickly.

Branwen sang softly as she worked, her melody weaving through the air as she touched the vines with reverence.

"That's beautiful," Rebecca said when Branwen paused for a moment.

"It's an old song. Older even than the stones that watch over this place, a melody spun from the earth by those who gave their lives for this land long ago."

"Why do you sing it?"

Branwen reached out and gently touched a vine bud. "It is for life, for growth, and for protection." She reached down to a smaller bud beneath, growing toward a healthier one. Branwen grasped it and snipped it away, its fragile life cut short to feed the stronger one.

"It is also for death, for the endings we must witness until we enter that last stage ourselves. The earth must be fed. Bounty only comes with sacrifice, and one day my bones and blood will feed this land." She turned and met Rebecca's gaze. "As will yours."

Branwen began to sing again. This time, the melody was different — deeper, more primal. It resonated in Rebecca's chest, making her heart beat in time with its rhythm. It grew stronger, as if the old woman channelled the power of the earth into the bud at her fingertips.

Beneath the soil, Rebecca could have sworn she heard something, a soft slithering, as if the roots of the vine were shifting, burrowing deeper into the earth to suck from the marrow of whatever dead things lay beneath.

Rebecca shook her head, trying to clear it. The lack of sleep and the strangeness of her new surroundings must be getting to her. And yet, as she turned back to her work, she found herself humming along with Branwen's song, the unfamiliar melody already etching itself into her memory.

CHAPTER 9

As the first rays of dawn crept over the horizon, Rebecca stirred in her bunk, her eyes fluttering open as she felt drawn back out to the vineyard before the others woke. She sat up, careful not to disturb the others sleeping, and peered out the window.

A thick blanket of mist clung to the vineyard, transforming the familiar rows of vines into a dreamlike landscape. Rebecca felt a strange pull, an almost primal need to be out there, to feel the damp earth beneath her feet and breathe in the crisp morning air.

She dressed quickly and quietly, slipping out of the bunkhouse and into the misty dawn. The grass was wet with dew, soaking the hem of her jeans as she made her way between the rows of vines. The world seemed hushed, holding its breath in anticipation of the new day.

As she rounded a bend in the path, Rebecca caught sight of a figure dancing gracefully among the vines, her arms sweeping up to the sky and then down to the earth in an ancient rhythm.

It was Isabelle, her silver hair catching the first rays of sunlight as she wove between the rows, her bare feet dancing over the ground. She must be so cold, and yet Rebecca could see no trace of discomfort as the woman moved with a light smile, her lips moving in something like a prayer. To the vines perhaps, or the morning sun. Whatever it was, Rebecca stood transfixed as Isabelle lightly brushed the vine buds with her fingertips.

After a moment, Isabelle turned, her eyes locking with Rebecca's even as she continued her dance.

"I'm sorry," Rebecca said. "I didn't mean to disturb you."

"Not at all." Isabelle smiled as she beckoned Rebecca over with a wave of her hand. "Come, join me. You can learn one of our most cherished traditions — of course, only women and children can dew dance like this."

Rebecca hesitated for a moment, then walked towards Isabelle, curiosity overcoming her initial shyness. The bottom of Isabelle's trousers were soaked, and her bare feet stained green from the dew-laden grass.

"It's an ancient ritual, dancing barefoot at dawn, to collect the morning dew and distribute it amongst the vines. It connects us with the earth's energy and feeds something of ourselves in the droplets back to the ground."

The idea of dancing barefoot through the damp grass and wildflowers and soil seemed unusual, almost primitive. But there was something in Isabelle's eyes, a mix of challenge and invitation, that made Rebecca reach down and unlace her boots, take off her socks, and stand barefoot on the chill earth.

She took a deep breath and just stood there for a minute. It was as if all sensation was magnified. The cold moisture between her toes, the soft give of the earth beneath her feet, the prickle of grass against her soles.

"How… how do I dance?"

Isabelle smiled as she spun once again. "There are no rules, only patterns of earth and clouds and birds diving and soaring. Just move as you feel you want to. Let your body be free."

Rebecca bit back her immediate response, honed by

years in the city where such New Age nonsense was usually the domain of vegan yoga studios. She felt uncomfortable at first, but as Isabelle danced on, focused only on the vines and the rising sun, Rebecca swept one foot out in front of her, circling the dew and enjoying the sensation.

"That's it," Isabelle encouraged, her voice low and soothing. "Let your feet caress the earth as you would touch a lover. Explore the sensations."

Rebecca followed Isabelle's lead as they moved slowly between the vines, her movements becoming freer with each row. Each step brought new sensations. A patch of cool, damp moss. The rough texture of exposed roots. The earth seemed to pulse with life, responding to their gentle footfalls, and Rebecca couldn't help the smile that rose to her lips. She'd heard the phrase 'touch grass' before, but never truly experienced it in this visceral way.

Isabelle smiled at her rising joy. "Women have danced here for generations and the land remembers. Every step, every touch, every drop of dew or sweat or blood that falls upon it leaves an echo in the terroir. We become part of the land this way."

As they danced into the labyrinth section of the vineyard, Rebecca's toe caught on something hard protruding from the soil. She stumbled slightly and bent down to see what it was.

Her fingers brushed against something smooth and curved. With a gentle tug, she pulled it free from the earth.

It was a piece of bone, yellowed with age, its surface etched with strange, intricate patterns reminiscent of the runes on the gate to the restricted area. It looked like a piece of skull. Could it even be human?

Isabelle danced back to her and took the piece of bone, pressing it back into the soil with reverence. Her expression remained serene, but her eyes glinted with something unreadable. "Dancing is not the only way we honour the land. Our ancestors understood the power of sacrifice, of giving back to the earth that nurtures us. And so it must be."

Rebecca watched with a mixture of fascination and unease. Part of her wanted to recoil, to run back to the safety and familiarity of the city. But another side of her wanted to know more about these pagan practices that gave the vineyard such energy and mystery. It was all so far from her London life but, with every day here, she thought perhaps she understood her sister a little more.

Isabelle stood and brushed the dirt from her hands. "Come. We must complete the dance while the dew is still fresh."

As they resumed their movements through the vines, Rebecca found her steps falling naturally into a rhythm with Isabelle's. Not quite matching her, but following so closely, it was as if something bound their movements together. Isabelle hummed a variation of the haunting melody Branwen had sung, her voice a part of the morning mist and the sound of the world waking.

Rebecca quietly hummed along, the unfamiliar tune feeling strangely right on her lips. With each step, each note, she felt herself sinking deeper into the rhythm of the land, part of something vast and ancient, and a smile played about her lips.

How could she have thought she lived a real life back in London? This was truly living. Her skin thrummed with the sensation of the chill and the cold and her connection to the earth.

The sun climbed higher and soon burned away the morning mist. As the golden light touched the vines, Isabelle turned and raised her arms to the sky, closing her eyes as if greeting the day. A ray of gold turned her hair into a halo and lifted the years from her skin, and Rebecca wondered if there was some kind of fountain of youth buried deep in the soil.

After a few minutes of silent reverence, Isabelle turned, her smile almost innocently happy. She gestured out over the land before them, and Rebecca realised with a start that they were on the highest rise of the property. Below them, she could see the shape of the spiralling labyrinth of vines, and the ancient staved fence behind the manor house.

"Do you feel it? The land is alive. It breathes, it speaks — if only we learn to listen."

Rebecca nodded. "I can understand why you love this place so much."

Isabelle bent to pick up a handful of soil. "Here, feel it."

Rebecca cupped her hands, and Isabelle poured the soil into them. It was cool and damp, rich and dark. As Rebecca ran her fingers through it, she could feel fragments of organic matter, the occasional small stone, the very essence of the earth itself.

"This soil has been nurtured for millennia." Isabelle's voice took on an almost reverent tone. "Fed by the seasons, by the toil of countless hands, by the sacrifice of those who came before us. Every vintage we produce is a testament to this legacy, and you are part of this now."

"Has your family owned this land for a long time?"

Isabelle shook her head. "There is no owning this land, only custodianship during the brief span of a human life, then it is passed on to another."

Her words seemed evasive, and Rebecca thought of the photograph she'd seen in the tasting room: A younger Isabelle, radiant with happiness, standing beside a man and a little girl.

"But you must have lived here a long time? I saw the photograph of you with your husband and daughter in the tasting room."

Isabelle was silent for a moment and her gaze flickered to the ancient stave fence before she spoke.

"Philip, my husband, and our daughter, Lily." She paused

and took a breath. "They have returned to the earth, as we all must, eventually. And so it must be." She turned to Rebecca and took her hand. "Now, come, you must be cold. Let's get back and warm up."

They walked down through the vines and as they reached the vineyard buildings, Nate emerged from the kitchen, two steaming mugs of coffee in his hands.

"Morning. I thought you might both need this. Cold work, dew dancing." His gaze lingered on Rebecca, a question in his eyes.

Isabelle took one mug, inhaling the rich aroma deeply before taking a sip. Rebecca accepted the other gratefully, the warmth seeping into her hands.

"Rebecca is a natural, Nate. Why don't you show her more of the biodynamic preparations today?"

Nate's eyes widened slightly. "If you're sure."

Isabelle turned to Rebecca, her smile warm but her gaze holding a hint of challenge. "If you're interested, of course? It's fascinating, truly at the heart of what we do here, but it's not for everyone."

Rebecca felt a thrill of excitement mixed with a touch of apprehension. This seemed more than just a simple invitation. It was a test that would take her deeper into the mysteries of Standing Stone Cellars.

"I'd love to learn. Thanks for the opportunity."

Isabelle smiled as she nodded with approval. "Excellent. I'll leave it with you both then. Let me know how it goes."

Rebecca headed back to the bunkhouse for a hot shower, mug of coffee in hand, smiling at the possibility of the day ahead.

Isabelle watched Rebecca walk away, the young woman's steps still enlivened by the dance. It had been a surprise to find her so gracefully accepting of the dew dance, but of course, the land called those it needed. Who was she to question the wisdom of the Horned God?

Nate put a hand on her arm. "Are you sure you want to reveal so much? She can't be ready."

"Better to know as soon as possible." Isabelle turned to Nate, and she felt the familiar, aching fatigue sink deeper into her bones, as if the years themselves were vines, tightening around her spine, heavy with the weight of too many seasons. "You know how long I've searched. Time is running out. You know this to be true. Will you teach her?"

Nate placed a gentle kiss on Isabelle's cheek. "Of course, I'll try, but if she rejects the teaching?"

Isabelle took a deep breath, her lips thinning as her expression hardened. "Then the land will have its due."

CHAPTER 10

LATER THAT DAY, REBECCA met Nate at the door of the preparation shed. They had only entered briefly on the initial tour, and a sense of anticipation rose within her as Nate unlocked the heavy wooden door. It creaked open and the smell of herbs and earth and a metallic tang emanated from the dark interior.

Nate stepped inside, and Rebecca followed, her eyes adjusting to the dim light. Bundles of herbs hung from the rafters in front of rough wooden shelves filled with wooden boxes marked with rune symbols, and rows of glass jars filled with different liquids, some with murky silt obscuring lumps of material inside.

Nate walked to the back of the room. "You only saw part of this on the first day."

He pushed open another door, hidden in the shadows, and Rebecca followed him through. The space beyond was far larger than she expected, a cavernous area that seemed to stretch impossibly far given the size of the shed they'd just left. Only one side was roofed, while the other opened to the sky, allowing shafts of sunlight to pierce through, illuminating motes of dust that danced in the air. It smelled of earth and sweet decay, and something else, something metallic and primal.

Huge wooden boxes stood on one side, each filled with organic matter at different stages of decomposition. Some of the compost heaps steamed gently in the cool air; others were full of rich, dark earth. A series of large bins stood nearby and Rebecca recognised crushed eggshells alongside bleached bones of various sizes and shapes, twisted cow horns, and what looked like the wrinkled, leathery remains of cow stomachs. She pushed down her sense of unease as Nate explained.

"This is where we do the real work. It takes some getting used to, but every element here plays a crucial role in nurturing the vines and infusing our wine with the essence of the land."

Nate led her to a curious contraption in the centre of the room. The large wooden barrel was mounted on a sturdy frame, its weathered surface etched with runic symbols.

"This is our dynamiser, used to stir and enliven our preparations, all according to the principles of biodynamics. We dilute it further before spraying it on the vines at times dictated by the celestial calendar. This batch has water from our sacred spring, mixed with a preparation of yarrow flowers fermented in a stag's bladder."

Nate moved around the shed and gathered various ingredients. He crushed eggshells with practiced ease, mixed them with finely ground quartz, and carefully measured out portions of other materials.

"Each preparation serves a specific purpose. Horn manure for root growth, horn silica for photosynthesis, yarrow for potassium, chamomile for calcium, stinging nettle as a general tonic. Almost all of this is grown and gathered from the vineyard or surrounding land, keeping the whole thing a closed system."

Rebecca listened with fascination. There was a poetry to the complex dance of elements, more like alchemy than agriculture.

Nate walked to a shelf and selected a small vial filled with dark liquid. The glass was scratched and dull with age, and the shape reminiscent of perfume bottles used in Roman times.

"We'll also add a few drops of this, distilled from plants growing in the most ancient area of the vineyard."

Rebecca wanted to ask more about the off-limit area but remembered his negative reaction to Asha's questions. Perhaps if she could earn Nate's trust, he might share more without her needing to ask.

Nate poured a few drops from the vial into the barrel, and the dark stain spread through the water until it disappeared. He grasped the handle attached to the barrel. "Now, we stir."

He turned the handle, slowly at first, then with increasing speed. The water in the barrel swirled, forming a vortex with a froth of rapidly moving water.

"We stir in one direction for about a minute," Nate explained, his muscles straining with the effort. "Then we abruptly change direction."

He reversed the motion and the smooth walls of the vortex collapsed into frothing turbulence. "This creates a moment of chaos, and it is in this chaos that the preparation is potentised."

As Nate continued to turn the handle, a new vortex formed, spinning in the opposite direction. The process continued, a hypnotic dance of creation and destruction.

"Your turn." Nate stepped back from the dynamiser.

Rebecca hesitated, then stepped forward, timing her movements with the handle and picking up where Nate had stopped, keeping the dynamiser going.

"That's it," he encouraged. "Feel the rhythm. Let it flow through you."

Rebecca fell into the pattern, stirring for a minute, then abruptly changing direction. With each turn, she felt more connected to the swirling liquid, as if it were an extension of her body.

"The vortex draws down cosmic forces," Nate explained, his voice seeming to come from far away. "The moment of chaos releases them into the preparation. We're not just stirring water. We're weaving the very fabric of creation, which we then give back to the earth. Some use mechanical dynamisers, but we believe it's important for the human element to be part of the process. This is the old way, the true way."

Rebecca's muscles strained on the reversal of the turn, muscles she had rarely used back in the city, and it felt good to use her body to help the vineyard.

"Listen," Nate whispered. "Can you hear it?"

At first, Rebecca heard nothing but the sloshing of water. Then, gradually, she noticed a low, rhythmic pulsing that seemed to emanate up from the barrel, drawn from the earth itself. It resonated in her chest, syncing with her heartbeat.

"Yes, I think I can."

Nate smiled, his eyes glinting in the dim light. "The land is singing, and it will share its secrets if you open your mind to it."

Rebecca's arms now burned with the effort of stirring, but she couldn't stop. The vortex grew stronger, the chaos moments more violent. With each turn, she felt herself sinking deeper into a trance-like state.

As she gazed down into the swirling water, images began to form.

Flashes of ancient ritual, of blood-soaked soil, and vines writhing as if they were alive. Rebecca saw herself dancing among the vines, her feet sinking into the earth, and then in the shadows, she saw Grace, her sister's face transformed into something wild and inhuman, her skin a mottled green and brown as if she were a living part of the earth.

Rebecca gasped and stepped back, her heart hammering at the vision.

Her brain must have reacted to some kind of chemical vapour from the preparation, along with the rhythmic trance of spinning. It wasn't real, she knew, but she couldn't get the image of Grace from her head.

With a final, violent turn, the vortex collapsed.

The water in the barrel settled, changing colour to a rich mahogany with a shimmer of crimson.

"That's enough for now," Nate said as he watched her reaction with curiosity. "It can be intense the first time, and this batch is done, anyway."

A shout came from outside. "Nate! Can you come and look at this?"

He sighed. "Duty calls. I won't be a minute."

As she waited, Rebecca noticed a collection of oddly shaped hooks hung from one wall, their tips wickedly sharp. They looked like gaffs on fishing boats, used to haul the biggest fish over the side. But what large animals might they be needed for here?

Nearby, a pile of animal skulls and bones lay waiting to be used in the preparations, next to what looked like a mask made of bark and vines twisted into horns.

Rebecca's heart still raced. The shed suddenly felt oppressive as shadows shifted in the corners of her vision, and the smell intensified, making her almost giddy. She needed to get out of here, into the fresh air away from the shed, but she didn't want Nate to realise her discomfort.

As she tried to calm herself, Rebecca noticed something on the far wall of the shed, partially hidden behind a stack of crates.

She walked over to look more closely.

It was an intricate mural made from stone and leaves and fragments of bone, daubed with a dark stain. A group of figures danced among ancient vines before a group of standing stones. At the centre stood a sinister horned figure, dripping with blood. At its feet, a bound creature, its face turned away, clearly some kind of sacrifice.

Rebecca bent closer.

The curve of the back, the long hair. Was that a young woman?

Nate's footsteps came from the outer room.

Rebecca spun away and pretended to study the shelf of preparation bottles to one side, attempting to calm her thudding heart as he strode back into the room.

"Right, that's enough for today. You did well."

He held the door for her and she gratefully left the shed, emerging into the dusk.

The sun was setting, painting the sky in shades of blood and wine, as she made her way back to the bunkhouse. Rebecca felt the back of her neck prickling and glanced back at the preparation shed, half-expecting to see a shadowy horned figure watching her.

But there was nothing there — just the gathering dusk and the vast, silent rows of vines.

CHAPTER 11

THE DAYS AT STANDING Stone Cellars blended into one another, each sunrise bringing with it a new set of tasks that slowly became familiar to Rebecca. She had emailed her manager and asked for extended leave, and soon she no longer thought of London. The vineyard's rhythm settled into her bones, a primal beat that pulsed with the rising and setting of the sun, the waxing and waning of the moon.

Most mornings she worked alongside Branwen, the elderly woman's gnarled hands moving with grace amongst the vines. Under her guidance, Rebecca learned to read the language of the plants, to understand the subtle shifts in their leaves and the meaning behind each tendril's reach.

"You see here?" Branwen said one morning, her fingers tracing the curve of a vine. "It's reaching for the sun, yes, but also for something deeper. The vines carry the wisdom of seasons long past. They remember, even as we forget."

As Rebecca worked, pruning and tending to the vines, she hummed Branwen's melodies, the haunting tunes rising almost unbidden. Sometimes, in the quietest moments, she could have sworn she heard the vines humming back, a soft rustle that was more feeling than sound.

On days when the vines needed less attention, Rebecca worked in the preparation room, assisting Nate as he taught her more about biodynamic practices. She rearranged the shelves so she could no longer see the disturbing mural and tried to forget it was even there.

While they worked in different areas, Rebecca couldn't help but observe her fellow newcomers, each finding their place within the vineyard's ecosystem as the weeks passed.

Asha remained a distant figure, more often glimpsed through windows of the main building than seen among the vines. Her carefully manicured nails and pristine clothes stood in stark contrast to the manual work of the vineyard. When she did venture into the vineyard, it was to make a quick video for social media before returning to the internet connection in the office.

Liam had taken to the vineyard's physical labour with a quiet intensity that bordered on obsession. He was a constant presence among the vines, starting early and finishing late, eating and falling into bed exhausted every night. He rarely spoke, but in the set of his shoulders and the careful precision of his work, Rebecca sensed he found solace in the repetitive tasks, as if each vine he tended was a step away from whatever shadowed his past.

Helen still bunked in the main block, and her enthusiasm about the vineyard was seemingly boundless. She flitted through the vineyard like a hummingbird, her notebook never far from her hand, its pages filling rapidly with sketches of plants and scribbled observations.

"Oh, Rebecca!" she would frequently exclaim, her eyes wide with excitement. "Did you know that the yarrow growing between the vines is not just beautiful, but also attracts beneficial insects? And over here, I've found a new patch of wild chamomile. Perhaps you and Nate could use it in the preparations?"

And then there was Ben.

Rebecca found her gaze drawn to him more and more often, noting the play of muscles beneath his shirt as he worked on the vineyard's equipment. Their eyes would sometimes meet across the rows of vines, a shared smile or a raised eyebrow speaking volumes.

It started small — a brush of hands as they reached for the same tool, the warmth of his arm against hers as they stood side by side, listening to Nate's instructions, or sitting together at dinner.

But soon, Rebecca found herself looking forward to these brief moments of contact, each one sending a thrill through her that had nothing to do with the vibrant energy of the vineyard.

One afternoon, as they worked together to repair a stubborn irrigation pipe, Ben's hand lingered on her arm a moment longer than necessary.

"You're getting the hang of this pretty quickly. Must be all that practical architect training?"

Rebecca felt a flush rise to her cheeks, one that had nothing to do with the afternoon sun. "Oh, I don't know about that." She leaned slightly into his touch. "I think it might have more to do with the teacher."

Their eyes met, and for a moment, the surrounding vineyard faded away as they drew closer.

Helen's excited voice calling from a nearby row broke the moment. "Oh my goodness, you simply must come and see this fascinating fungus!"

As they laughed together and turned towards Helen's call, Ben's hand slipped from Rebecca's arm, but the warmth of his touch lingered.

Yet even as she revelled in the growing connection with Ben and the satisfying rhythm of vineyard life, a part of Rebecca remained alert. The strange mural in the preparation shed, the visions in the dynamiser, and the unsettling intensity in Nate's eyes when he spoke of the land's power — all these things lurked at the edges of her mind. Despite the serene surface of Standing Stone vineyard, deeper and darker currents flowed beneath.

One afternoon, Ben approached Rebecca as she finished tying off a row of vines.

"Fancy a change of scenery? I need to check the equipment in the fermentation shed, and I don't think you've had a chance to see that part of the process yet."

Rebecca nodded and brushed the soil from her hands, smiling as she anticipated time with him away from curious eyes. "Of course, I'd love to."

They walked close together, hands almost touching, and entered the fermentation shed, where the earthy scent of the vineyard gave way to a yeasty aroma with an underlying tang of alcohol.

A network of pipes snaked across the ceiling and down the walls, connecting a series of concrete vats.

Ben gestured at the closest one. "These are where the wild yeast begins its work, converting sugar into alcohol. It's a delicate process—one where nature takes the lead. Standing Stone doesn't add commercial yeast, it's all about using the wild strains, those that live on the grape skins and in the air around the vineyard. The very essence of terroir. But every ferment is different, so it's risky and unpredictable, but that's what makes biodynamics so interesting and the resulting vintage so unusual."

They walked on into the bottling area, settling into a comfortable rhythm as Ben explained the intricacies of each piece of equipment. Rebecca absorbed the information, her architect's mind already sketching out possible improvements and adaptations. There were ways this place could be reorganised to make it more efficient, although she wondered whether efficiency was desired here, when the more elemental nature of the vineyard was the focus.

Ben stretched up to check one of the gauges on the bottling line. "I love working here, but it's a long way from home."

"Where's home for you?" Rebecca asked.

"Northumberland. Have you been?"

Rebecca shook her head, suddenly aware of how little she knew about her own country. "I've heard it's beautiful."

Ben nodded. "You should see it — miles of untamed beaches, cliffs that look like they've been carved by giants. The sea there, it's not like anywhere else. One moment it's calm as glass, the next it's a maelstrom that could swallow you whole."

His eyes took on a faraway look, and Rebecca could almost see the windswept shores he described and feel the salt spray on her face.

"It's in my blood. No matter where I go, part of me is always there, feet in the sand, listening to the gulls and the crash of waves. What about you? Where's home?"

Rebecca hesitated. The word 'home' was so loaded with expectation about happy families and shared moments. She thought of her flat back in London, of the life she'd left behind, and the fact that her parents didn't even know she was here.

A sharp sudden crack suddenly echoed through the facility, followed by the sound of liquid dripping onto the floor.

Ben's head snapped around, his expression shifting to focused concern in an instant. "Damn. That sounds like one of the bottles on the riddling rack. Come on, we'd better check it out."

As they walked towards the source of the sound, Rebecca felt a mixture of relief at avoiding the difficult question and regret at the lost moment of connection. She followed Ben, watching his confident stride as he navigated the maze of equipment, and wondered just how much of herself she was ready to reveal.

They turned a corner and walked over to the row of wooden riddling racks filled with glass bottles. One on the end of the row had indeed burst, and shards of glass lay in a frothy pool of sparkling wine across the stone floor, as the sharp scent of citrus and elderflower filled the air.

As they worked together to clean up the mess, Rebecca asked, "So why did you leave Northumberland if you love it so much?"

"Perhaps we don't know what we have until we lose it, but as a teenager, I was desperate to leave and go traveling. I spent a summer in Burgundy in France. I was drifting, unsure what I wanted to do with my life, and I ended up working at this tiny family-owned vineyard. Very prestigious, not that I knew anything about that at the time."

As Ben spoke, his hands moved expressively, as if painting pictures in the air. Rebecca could almost see the sun-drenched hills of France, smell the rich earth and ripening grapes.

"They did everything the old way. Hand-picking the grapes, foot-stomping some of the batches. They even had this ancient basket press. Must have been at least a century old. It creaked and groaned like it was alive. The way the people there connected with the land changed something in me and I stayed."

His voice took on a reverent tone. "There was this old vintner, Jean-Pierre. He could tell you the exact row a grape came from just by tasting it. Said the vines spoke to him." Ben shook his head, a smile playing over his lips. "I thought he was mad at first, but by the end of that summer, I could hear them too. The whispers of the vines, the song of the seasons."

Rebecca nodded. "I think I know what you mean."

"It was there I first heard about Standing Stone. Jean-Pierre mentioned it one night over dinner, with perhaps a hint of jealousy about the awards the vineyard has won. He said it was one of the few places outside of France that truly understood the soul of wine-making. That they were doing something special here."

Ben turned to Rebecca, his eyes alight with passion. "And he was right. The biodynamic practices are not just about making wine. They're about connecting with the earth in a way that's been lost in so much of modern viticulture. I want to be part of taking the movement forward."

Rebecca smiled in recognition at his pull of ambition. It echoed the dreams she'd had of creating spaces that would transform people's lives. Those dreams had been crushed in the city, but perhaps this time away might rekindle them again.

"I know what you mean. In architecture, we're always trying to find a balance between form and function, between the built environment and the natural world, retaining the pillars of tradition, but also experimenting with new ideas."

Ben took her hand, his fingertips tracing a pattern on her palm. The intimate movement made her heart race. "Are you finding new ideas here?"

Rebecca nodded. "In the city, everything is angled and cornered. But out here, the lines are curved and organic. Even though most of the vines are in straight rows, there is the labyrinth section, and the way the vines twist as they grow, how they interact with the landscape. I'm starting to see how we could incorporate more natural forms into urban spaces. Green walls that mimic the growth patterns of vines, buildings that flow with the landscape instead of imposing themselves upon it."

Ben's face lit up. "It's the same with wine-making. We're not just producing a drink, we're creating an experience, a connection to the land and the seasons. It's art and science and maybe some magic all rolled into one perfect mouthful."

As Ben leaned towards her, Rebecca felt a warmth in her chest that had nothing to do with the day's exertions. She wanted to tell him about Grace and the real reason she'd come to Standing Stone.

But something held her back.

He seemed so entirely enthusiastic about the place, but there were still some aspects of the vineyard practices she questioned. How could she explain herself without sounding like a city girl who just didn't understand what she witnessed? He would think her ignorant and she couldn't bear that. Given his love of nature, Ben would also frown on her involvement in the destruction of trees in London.

A flush of shame washed over her. She pulled her hand out of his and turned away. "Are we done here? I promised to help Nate with some preparations."

"Almost." Ben looked disappointed as he put the cleaning equipment away, and Rebecca hoped she hadn't killed whatever it was between them too soon.

As they walked past one of the bottling machines, she noticed a drip of liquid coming from a loose component.

"Ben, is this a problem?"

He walked back and had a look. "Good catch. Let's take a look."

Together, they bent over the machine, their heads close as they examined the problematic part. Rebecca reached out, her fingers probing the metal connector. It was stubborn, refusing to budge despite her efforts.

"Here, let me try," Ben offered, his hand brushing against hers as he took over.

Rebecca stepped back slightly, watching as Ben's muscles strained against the resistant metal. Despite his strength, the part remained stubbornly in place.

"It's really stuck."

"Maybe if we both try together?" Rebecca suggested.

Ben nodded and they positioned themselves on either side of the connector, their hands overlapping as they gripped the metal.

"On three," Ben said. "One… two… three!"

They pulled together, their bodies working in unison. For a moment, nothing happened. Then, with a sudden give, the connector shifted.

The abrupt movement threw them off balance.

Rebecca stumbled backward, and Ben reached out instinctively to steady her. His arm wrapped around her waist, pulling her close.

Suddenly, they were face to face, bodies pressed together, breath mingling.

Rebecca could feel the solid warmth of Ben's chest against hers, see the flecks of gold in his hazel eyes. His gaze dropped to her lips, and she leaned in, drawn by an irresistible force.

The air between them crackled with tension, with possibility.

Rebecca's heart thundered in her chest, drowning out the ambient hum of the machinery. Ben's hand tightened slightly on her waist, and she could feel the slight tremor in his fingers.

Their lips were mere inches apart.

Rebecca's eyes fluttered closed, anticipation coiling in her stomach. She could feel the whisper of Ben's breath on her skin as he leaned in.

A sharp clang shattered the moment.

They jumped apart, startled by the sudden noise.

Ben's hand had knocked against a lever, setting off a chain reaction of moving parts.

"Careful!" Rebecca cried, reaching out to steady the shifting machinery.

But it was too late.

As Ben turned, his arm caught on the edge. There was a flash of silver, a muffled curse, and then — blood.

A lot of blood.

CHAPTER 12

Crimson drops spattered the stone floor, forming a stark line against the grey, a vivid streak that pulsed in the dim light.

Ben gripped his arm as blood welled up beneath his fingertips. "I'm okay. Just get the first aid kit."

He sank down to the floor, his back to the machine. The metallic scent of blood rose in the air, sharp and cloying. Rebecca could see Ben was struggling. The cut must be deep.

She rushed to a set of cupboards nearby marked with a green cross, and rifled through them, desperately looking for the first aid kit.

Footsteps approached from outside.

Nate appeared at the door. "Everything alright in here?"

"Ben had an accident. We need a first aid kit, quickly!"

Instead of rushing to help, Nate stood for a moment, his gaze fixed on Ben and the crimson streak of blood as it pulsed onto the floor, almost as if he willed it to pump faster and leave more of a stain. There was a drain nearby, where traces of the spilled wine still lingered. As the blood trailed towards it, Rebecca fleetingly wondered what lay beneath.

"Nate? The first aid kit?"

He blinked, as if coming out of a trance. "Yes, of course."

He reached into a cabinet above the cupboards, his

movements unhurried, retrieved the first aid kit and walked over to Ben with no sense of urgency.

Rebecca stood watching as Nate efficiently cleaned and bandaged Ben's wound. It seemed accidents were no rare occurrence here.

Isabelle appeared in the doorway. "Are you okay, Ben? What happened?"

Ben nodded, forcing a smile. "Yes, all good. Just a minor accident. Nate patched me up."

Isabelle's gaze lingered on the blood-stained floor for a moment before calling out, "Rebecca, would you mind helping me with something? If you're done here, of course."

Rebecca hesitated. She wanted to stay with Ben, to make sure he was truly okay, especially as she was partly to blame. But she didn't want to refuse Isabelle.

Ben gave a reassuring smile. "Go, I'm fine. Nate can help me clean up here."

Still, Rebecca hesitated. There was something in the air, a tension she couldn't quite identify. The way Nate looked at the blood, the careful neutrality in Isabelle's expression — it set her nerves on edge.

But what could she say? That she was afraid to leave Ben alone with Nate? That she suspected something sinister in a simple request for help? It all sounded paranoid, even in her own mind.

"Come on." Isabelle beckoned from the door. "I'm sure the boys can manage without you."

Ben waved her away, so Rebecca followed Isabelle out and on towards the parking area.

A battered pickup truck rumbled into view, its engine sputtering to a stop as it pulled up beside them. The farmer who climbed out was a weathered man, his face lined with age and hardship.

"Afternoon, Tom. What have you got for me?"

Tom walked around to the back of the truck. "A fine

specimen. Taken early this morning up on the Quantocks. He's still warm."

As the tailgate dropped, Rebecca's breath caught in her throat.

A magnificent red deer lay in the back, his coat a deep russet, stained with blood. There was an incision from the rib cage to the pelvis and a pile of entrails lay steaming next to it in a metal bucket. His antlers had been severed and rested against his back.

Rebecca had never been this close to a deer before, let alone such a huge dead one, but she certainly enjoyed eating venison. It was confronting as hell to think what must happen next. Once again, she felt like an outsider who knew nothing about the countryside or the animals and people who made her lifestyle possible in the city.

"Beautiful, isn't he?" Isabelle reached out and stroked the stag's haunch. "If we want to eat meat, we must slaughter first. His life was given to bring life to others. And so it must be." She pointed at a large wheeled cart with a mini crane and hanging straps in the corner of the parking area. "Can you wheel that over?"

As Rebecca manoeuvred the cart over the gravel back to the truck, she noticed dark stains on its metal sides. Old blood, she realised, and suppressed a shudder. This was a completely normal part of rural life, and as a meat eater, she was a hypocrite for feeling any judgment.

Isabelle and Tom expertly slung the deer and hoisted it out and onto the cart, along with the entrails.

Tom carried the antlers out and rested them against a nearby wall. "You need any more help?"

Isabelle shook her head. "No, you get off now. I have a new helper today."

A cold certainty rose within Rebecca as she realised she was the helper, unless she made a fuss and excused herself. But she wanted Isabelle's approval, so she pushed down the unease.

Isabelle wheeled the cart towards a low stone building in back of the kitchens and Rebecca hesitated a moment before following.

"I'd love you to help with the butchery," Isabelle said, her voice calm and reassuring. "It's a necessary part of life, after all. We don't kill for sport; we kill to sustain. Hunting is strictly regulated by the season, and it helps keep the deer population healthy. It prevents overgrazing, which can destroy habitats for many species, not just the deer."

Rebecca nodded, trying to absorb the information.

"City people rarely understand," Isabelle continued, as each second took them another metre closer to the door ahead. "They see the end product, the neatly packaged meat in the supermarket, but they don't see the process. Out here, we honour the animal. The meat feeds our families, the hide is tanned for leather, and we use the bones and antlers as part of the biodynamic practices on the vineyard. Nothing is wasted."

Rebecca reached out to touch the stag. It was still warm, its coat rough and dense. "It looks so healthy and well."

Isabelle nodded. "This stag lived a good life in the wild. It wasn't penned in or fed unnatural food. Its end was swift and as humane as possible, and there is honour in being part of the way its body is used after death."

They reached the door of the hut. "You wanted to know more about our practices here, so will you help me?"

Rebecca took a deep breath, wondering if her time at the vineyard might be about to end in humiliation. This was so far removed from her life in London, from the sterile, pre-packaged world she'd left behind. Part of her wanted to run, to flee back to the safety of the city where meat came in plastic wrapping, sanitised and disconnected from the violence of its origin.

Would she just vomit at the sight of blood, or faint, or embarrass herself?

But a glimmer of curiosity sparked within, a part that seemed to grow stronger with each day she spent at the vineyard. Rebecca was drawn to the primal nature of what Isabelle offered. This was real. This was life and death and the turning of seasons all bound up in one bloody package.

She nodded. "Yes, I want to help."

Isabelle pushed open the door to reveal a sterile, clean room, the stark white a contrast to the rustic stone exterior and the organic shapes and colours of the vineyard. Another sling and various hooks hung from the ceiling, while a rack on the wall held knives of all sizes, saws, and cleavers. At the back of the room, there was a reinforced door to a refrigeration unit.

Together, they pushed the cart in and to one side of a large metal table, slightly sloped toward a drain in the middle.

"I'm glad you want to help. We use every part of the animal. The meat will feed us for days, and the offal—heart, liver, kidneys—will become pâté. The bones will go into our stocks and stews and into our biodynamic preparations, and we render the fat for candles."

Rebecca swallowed down her rising nausea. "And the blood?"

"A gift to the vines, to ensure a bountiful harvest. The land will have its due, and so it must be."

Isabelle deftly hooked up the stag's back legs and used the hoist to hang the carcass, before putting on a heavy apron and pulling on a pair of thick rubber gloves. The older woman's movements were practiced, almost ritualistic in their precision, as she placed a large copper vat beneath the stag's head.

"Here." Isabelle handed Rebecca a similar pair of gloves and a waterproof apron like the one she was wearing. "You'll need these, especially the first time."

The apron was stiff and, as Rebecca slipped it over her head, she smelled copper and the scent of something earthy.

She swallowed hard, steeling herself for what was to come.

Isabelle ran her hand along the deer's flank in an almost reverent caress. "Beautiful creature," she murmured. "Thank you for your sacrifice."

She reached for a long, wickedly sharp knife and held it out to Rebecca. "Would you like to make the first cut?"

"I… I've never done it before. I don't know how."

Isabelle smiled. "There's always a first time, and it will be memorable. Don't worry, I'll show you."

Rebecca hesitated, her hand trembling slightly as she reached for the knife. Its weight was surprising, the handle worn smooth from years of use.

Isabelle drew her hand along the stag's throat. "Start here and make a cut to open the carotid. Gravity does the work for us then, and proper bleeding improves the quality of the meat and prevents it from spoiling."

Rebecca bent and placed the edge of the knife against the deer's neck, feeling the give of the flesh beneath. It was dead already. She wouldn't be killing it, but the action still seemed brutal.

"The blade is sharp, and the skin there is thin, so you just need to slice gently." Isabelle's tone was encouraging.

Rebecca took another breath as her vision narrowed to take in each individual hair on the deer's carcass. She didn't need to do this. She could just walk away right now. But what if she passed this test? What might she learn next?

She leaned in and sliced the knife across the stag's neck.

Warm blood gushed out, spattering into the copper vat. The metallic scent filled her nostrils, making her head swim as a few droplets splashed onto her gloves.

Isabelle smiled with pride as the blood began to drain out of the carcass. So much blood.

"I'll skin it now. It helps the drainage." Isabelle took over, her movements swift and sure as she skinned the stag. The wet sound of flesh separating from hide filled the room, punctuated by the soft scrape of the knife against bone.

As Isabelle worked with expert strokes, Rebecca found herself drawn into the process despite her initial revulsion. There was a strange beauty to it, a raw honesty in a practice that humans had performed for millennia, without which civilisation might never have flourished.

The carcass opened up beneath Isabelle's skilled hands, revealing the intricate architecture of muscle and bone as more blood drained from it.

As she worked, Isabelle sang a low, haunting melody similar to the songs Branwen sang in the vineyard, but with a darker edge, a primal rhythm that seemed to resonate with the very bones of the earth.

"The vines grow hungry," Isabelle whispered at the end of the song. "We must feed them well, and in turn, they reward us with bounty." She finished skinning. "Now for the real work. Sometime we hang the stag for longer, but if we butcher this now, we can have venison for dinner."

Isabelle swung the stag up and onto the butchering table with the hoist and then reached for a smaller, curved knife. "We'll start by removing the shoulders and haunches."

She demonstrated the first cut, her movements precise and almost graceful, then handed the knife to Rebecca, guiding her hand. "Like this. Feel for the joint, then let the blade do the work."

As Rebecca made the cut, she felt a strange thrill course through her. The knife sliced through flesh and sinew with surprising ease, revealing the intricate layers of muscle beneath. In many ways, it was structural and architectural, each level building on the next to make an animal that could move and live with ease in the natural environment.

"Good." Isabelle nodded approvingly. "You have a natural touch."

They worked in tandem, Rebecca following Isabelle's lead as they separated each cut of meat.

Rebecca found herself falling into a rhythm as her initial squeamishness faded. There was something meditative about the process, a primal connection to the cycle of life and death.

"In the old days," Isabelle said, "butchery was sacred work. Each cut was a prayer, each drop of blood an offering."

"I can see why. It's… beautiful, in a way."

As they continued, Isabelle would pause sometimes, her fingertips tracing intricate patterns on the exposed flesh reminiscent of those Rebecca had seen around the vineyard. "These are old sigils, passed down through generations. They honour the animal's spirit and bind its essence to the land."

She began to sing again, and this time, Rebecca hummed along, the eerie melody seeming to resonate with the marrow in the bones they worked on.

Suddenly, Rebecca's knife slipped, nicking her finger through the glove.

A drop of her blood welled up and dripped onto the table, mingling with the stag's.

Before Rebecca could react, Isabelle dipped her finger into the mingled blood and formed another symbol across the stag's flank. The air in the room seemed to thicken, humming with an energy that made Rebecca's skin prickle.

"You are part of this sacrifice now, and the land will sense your essence in it. The vines will reward you. But step back now, you're tired. I'll finish the rest. Just watch me so you can learn for next time."

While Isabelle's actions were disturbing, her words gave Rebecca a sense of pride. If there was to be a next time, she must have passed this test. Perhaps she wasn't just a city girl after all. She wished Grace could see her here, learning more about the rural life her sister was so at home in.

She watched as Isabelle continued working, breaking down the carcass into smaller cuts that slowly became recognisable as something Rebecca might have bought in a butcher's shop.

When they finished, Rebecca stood back to survey their work.

The once-magnificent deer was now reduced to neatly arranged cuts of meat, piles of organs, and bones stripped clean. Nothing was wasted. Every part would feed the cycle of life and death that pulsed through Standing Stone vineyard.

Rebecca looked down at herself. She was stained with blood and other fluids, her gloves sticky with gore. Yet she felt strangely exhilarated, as if she had passed through some unseen barrier into a world more vital than the one she'd left behind.

They cleaned up and wrapped the various cuts, and then placed them inside the refrigeration unit, along with the copper vat of blood.

As they finished and hosed down the clean room, Isabelle turned to Rebecca. "You've done well. Go and clean yourself up, then join me in the main house for dinner at seven. Just the two of us. We'll have venison loin and a bottle of wine. I have something else you might be interested in... if you'd like to join me, of course?"

There was a weight to the invitation, a sense of significance that made Rebecca's pulse quicken.

"Yes, of course, I'd love that."

As she turned to leave, Rebecca caught sight of her reflection in a hanging blade. For a moment, in the warped surface, she thought she saw something behind her — a shadowed figure with antlered horns rising from its brow. She shook her head to clear it and walked out of the stone hut into the fresh air.

CHAPTER 13

A FEW HOURS LATER, Rebecca walked along the path up to the manor house, the one building she had not yet visited. It was Isabelle's private area, and only those invited could go inside.

It was a behemoth of weathered stone and leaded glass windows, a sprawling structure with parts dating back several centuries and newer additions grafted on like architectural scar tissue. Tendrils of green vines snaked up the walls, forcing their way between stones, as if the vineyard were trying to reclaim that which encroached on its land.

The manor gardens were a blend of careful cultivation and wild abandon. Neatly trimmed hedges gave way to tangled thickets, while patches of twisted plants she didn't recognise interrupted manicured flowerbeds.

The elaborate door had spiral and knot symbols carved into its weathered wood, and above them, a knocker of heavy bronze.

As Rebecca let it fall, the resulting boom echoed through the house and beyond, like the tolling of some eldritch bell.

A minute later, Isabelle pulled open the door, her silver hair glinting from the warm light within. The rich aroma of roasting meat came from inside, but underneath, there was a scent that made Rebecca think of freshly turned earth and things long buried.

"Come in. Dinner won't be long, but I want to show you something first. This way."

Isabelle led the way up a grand spiral staircase, hung with dusty portraits and more recent photos from the vineyard. A younger Isabelle smiled out from some, along with her handsome husband and little girl, but then in other photos, the man was absent, and then the girl was gone, too. They reached the landing and passed door after door, each one closed tight. It was a big house for one person.

At last, they came to a set of heavy double doors, and Isabelle pushed them open to reveal a magnificent library. Floor-to-ceiling shelves groaned under the weight of countless books, their leather spines cracked and faded with age, while other cases displayed more modern volumes.

"This is our collection on viticulture and biodynamics," Isabelle said proudly. "Some of these tomes date back centuries, and some were even written here, documenting the life cycle and seasons of Standing Stone."

"The *Codex Vitis.*" Isabelle pointed out a massive volume open on a lectern, its pages yellowed with age. It was covered in spidery writing and diagrams that seemed to shift and change as Rebecca looked at them.

Isabelle continued, "It contains the secrets of winemaking passed down from the Romans, and there is a whisper of older, darker knowledge within its pages." She walked over to one bookcase and bent down to a wide drawer. "I wanted to show you these—"

A bell tinkled from downstairs.

"Oh, that's dinner. We only have a few minutes, and we still need to choose some wine. I'll show you the drawings after we eat. Come. I think you'll like the wine cellar."

They descended the main stairs once more, then went down a narrow spiral staircase, the temperature dropping with each step. The wine cellar stretched out before them, a catacomb of bottles and barrels in racks with markings of each vintage.

As they walked through, Isabelle spoke of sun-drenched summers and bitter winters, of struggles against frost and bounties beyond imagining.

She pulled a dust-covered bottle from one rack. "This was the year of the great storm. Lightning struck our oldest oak, and the wine… well, it has a certain electricity to it, you might say." She placed it back on the rack. "We'll have a more recent Pinot Noir with the venison, I think."

As Isabelle navigated through the cellar, looking for a suitable vintage, Rebecca noticed an unusual door at the far end of the cellar.

It was ancient oak, its surface intricately carved with vines and grapes, twisting around a horned figure with its arms raised to the moon above. Aspects of it echoed the mural she'd seen in the preparation shed.

Isabelle picked a bottle and checked the label. "This will do nicely." The bell rang again. "Let's go up. We have much to discuss."

Rebecca took one last glance at the carved door, her curiosity roused, and followed Isabelle up to the grand dining room.

The food was delicious, the rich flavour of venison lingering on Rebecca's palate, expertly paired with the Pinot Noir that made her heady with its bouquet. She was truly eating and drinking local and sustainable food, and she was proud to have helped butcher the creature that now sustained her own body.

Isabelle talked of the various seasonal activities of the vineyard, and Rebecca shared aspects of her architectural career, skimming over personal stories of her family life. The conversation flowed as easily as the wine, and Rebecca found herself wanting to learn more from the older woman, who seemed to welcome her closer to the heart of the vineyard.

After dinner, Isabelle led the way back to the library, as the house creaked and sighed around them with the falling temperature of night.

The scent of old books and leather mingled with the fruity aroma of wine as Isabelle turned on some low lamps, casting a golden glow over the expanse of books. It was a heaven for book-lovers, indeed.

Isabelle returned to the wide drawer, and pulled out a sheaf of architectural plans, laying them on a mahogany desk nearby. "These were to be our future."

Rebecca leaned in and assessed the sweeping lines and bold design, dragging her architectural knowledge back up from her wine-induced haze. The plans showed an ambitious expansion of Standing Stone Cellars, with new planting areas stretched across nearby hillsides and a new event space that wound organically through the landscape.

Rebecca traced the lines with her fingertips. "It's a beautiful design, but why wasn't it built?"

Isabelle's expression darkened, and a shadow passed across her face like a storm cloud. "The architect didn't share my vision. He was bound by conventional thinking, too afraid to commune with the land and understand our customs." She paused for a long second. "He served the vines in other ways, though, as it must be."

There was something in Isabelle's tone that made Rebecca frown and she wondered where the architect might be now. Before she could dwell on it, Isabelle pressed on.

"But you understand, don't you? You've felt the pulse of the vines, you've heard its whispers." She met Rebecca's gaze. "And perhaps you've even seen its horned guardian?"

Rebecca nodded slowly. "Yes, I've seen him."

"With your architectural knowledge and affinity for the land, might you consider taking on this project? We need to expand our planting areas and create spaces for events, but in a manner that truly honours the land and our biodynamic principles."

Rebecca's heart raced at the prospect. This was an opportunity beyond anything she'd dared hope for. It would be a chance to apply her skills in a way that felt meaningful, and be connected to something greater than herself.

"I'd love to at least try. I'd need some time to go through the plans, and then I could present my ideas to you as a next step."

Isabelle smiled. "Excellent. Your skills are more valuable this way. You can start work in here tomorrow, instead of on the vines, and use the computer in the administration block for whatever you need." She glanced at her watch. "It's late. You better get back now. It's been a long day."

Isabelle showed her to the door and waved her out into the night.

As Rebecca made her way back to the bunkhouse, the vineyard seemed to pulse and sway around her. Whether from the wine or the intoxicating possibilities Isabelle had laid before her, she couldn't be sure.

Her fingertips brushed against the leaves of the vines as she walked, and she could have sworn they reached back, caressing her skin with a lover's touch. The night air was alive with whispers — the rustle of leaves, the chirp of insects, and underneath it all, a low, rhythmic chant that seemed to emanate from the earth itself.

For a moment, Rebecca thought of Grace, of the questions still unanswered.

But memories of the past slipped away like smoke, lost in the heady rush of new possibilities. There would be time later to search the vineyard records, to learn what the library held, and perhaps even to enter the mysterious door in the wine cellar. There were many secrets here, but Rebecca was one step closer to discovering more.

For now, she allowed herself to dream of sweeping designs that would honour the land and structures that would grow from the earth like living things.

Ben crouched in the shadows of the preparation shed as he watched Rebecca walk out of the manor house and along the edge of the vineyard towards the bunkhouse. Her footsteps wove slightly, and she hummed a strange melody as she disappeared into the darkness.

Part of him wanted to call out to her, to kiss her amongst the vines and perhaps even learn what she had been doing in there with Isabelle. But the words died in his throat, choked by the weight of his own secrets. She couldn't know why he was really there. It would put her in too much danger.

Shaking off his doubts, Ben stood and began to work at the lock of the preparation shed.

CHAPTER 14

THE WEEKS FOLLOWING REBECCA'S dinner with
Isabelle passed in a whirlwind of activity. Each day, she woke
with the sun, her mind already buzzing with ideas and plans
for the vineyard's expansion.

The library became her second home, its shelves offering
secrets of ancient techniques and sacred geometry that she
carefully incorporated into her designs.

The original plans were a starting point, but she infused
them with her own vision, one that honoured the land's
unique energy while pushing the boundaries of conventional
design. She hummed the strange vineyard melodies as she
sketched spiral pathways to mimic the growth patterns of
vines and event spaces that seemed to grow organically from
the earth.

As she worked, Rebecca felt a growing connection to
Standing Stone Cellars. This was more than a job now; it
was a kind of calling. She wanted her designs to be perfect,
not just for her own pride, but as a way of giving back to
the community that welcomed her, and to Isabelle, who had
placed such trust in her abilities.

The days blurred together, marked by the steady progress
of her plans and the subtle changes in the vineyard as the
young leaves unfurled. Although she didn't work amongst

them every day, Rebecca often took a break from her plans to walk through the vine rows, enjoying the play of light and how the landscape shifted and changed with each passing day.

Her focus didn't go unnoticed. Isabelle would often stop by the library, her eyes sparkling with approval as she reviewed Rebecca's latest sketches. "These are wonderful. You see the land as it truly is, as it wants to be."

But it wasn't all work.

In stolen moments between drafting sessions and site surveys, Rebecca found herself drawn closer to Ben. Their encounters were brief, but charged with an energy that left her breathless. A brush of hands as they passed in the vineyard, a shared smile over dinner in the common room, a lingering glance across the tasting room, but the kiss that had almost been was only a memory.

One evening, as Rebecca was heading back to the bunkhouse after a long day of work, she quite literally ran into Ben. He steadied her with firm hands on her waist, and for a moment, neither of them moved.

"You're working too hard." Ben's voice was low and intimate in the gathering twilight. "All work and no play, you know what they say. Besides, I've missed you."

Rebecca felt a blush rise to her cheeks. "There's just so much to achieve here. I want the plans to be perfect."

Ben's hand moved to her cheek, his touch feather-light. "They will be, I'm sure, but don't forget to live a little too. The vineyard isn't just about work, it's about life and celebration."

As if on cue, the sound of distant laughter drifted across the vines, and Rebecca realised with a start that she'd almost forgotten about the upcoming Beltane festival. She'd been so focused on her work that the passage of time had become abstract.

"You're right." She leaned into Ben's touch. "Maybe I do need a break."

"Beltane is the perfect time to let loose, to really become part of life here. What do you say? Will you join me — us — for the celebration tomorrow?"

There was a promise in his words, and Rebecca nodded, caught up in the warmth of his gaze and the hint that their almost-kiss might turn into something more. "Yes, I'd like that."

As Ben walked her back to the bunkhouse, his hand finding hers in the deepening darkness, Rebecca felt a thrill of anticipation. Beltane might turn out to be more than just a celebration of the vineyard and the community.

The next morning, Rebecca stirred in her bunk as the cracks of sleep widened into consciousness. What was that noise?

At first, she thought the pulsing rhythm was the remnant of a dream, but as she blinked away the haze of slumber, the sound persisted. A steady, primal beat vibrated through the very foundations of the bunkhouse.

She sat up, her bare feet touching the cool wooden floor. The other bunks were empty, her fellow workers already risen and gone.

How long had she slept?

The quality of light filtering through the curtains suggested the sun was high, far later than her usual dawn rising, evidence that she really was exhausted from too many hours working in the library.

The drumming grew louder and more insistent as Rebecca dressed. She could feel it in her chest, in her bones, as if the earth was awakening to some ancient call.

She stepped outside, and the transformation took her breath away.

The vineyard, usually an array of greens and browns, had exploded into colour. Vibrant ribbons in shades of crimson, emerald, and marigold fluttered from the vines, dancing in the spring breeze. Garlands of wildflowers wound their way along fences and trellises, their sweet perfume mingling with the earthy scent of the vines.

The beating of drums grew stronger, and now she could hear other instruments joining in — the haunting wail of a fiddle and the bright jangle of tambourines. The music wove through the air, drawing her on.

Rebecca followed the sound to the area in front of the tasting room, where a crowd of vineyard workers and others from the community gathered.

Isabelle stood before them, her silver hair adorned with a crown of spring flowers. As she raised her hands, the music and drums fell silent.

"Welcome, one and all. Today, we celebrate Beltane, the midpoint between the spring equinox and the summer solstice. A time of renewal, of fertility, a time when the veil between our world and the other grows thin. Today, we honour the land that sustains us, and we ask for its blessing on our vines."

Rebecca had heard of Beltane, but had presumed it was a quaint historical footnote or a reason for modern pagans to dance around a maypole in ridiculous clothes. But here, it was clearly a living tradition with roots that ran deep into the soil, a celebration for a close-knit community who depended on this place.

Isabelle continued, "Our rituals are a covenant with the land. A promise renewed each year. We give of ourselves, and in return, the earth gives us its bounty. Now, we have much to prepare for the feast tonight. Let us begin!"

The crowd dispersed, breaking into smaller groups with practiced efficiency. Rebecca found herself swept along towards a field where a massive pile of logs was taking shape.

"Here." Nate appeared at her side, handing her a log. "Every hand helps build the fire."

Rebecca took the wood, its rough bark scraping against her palms. As she walked over to place it on the growing pile, she noticed the vineyard's runic symbols etched into it. From her reading, she now recognised them as old local magic, prayers to the earth written in a language older than words.

She placed her log on the pile while others brought more wood. Slowly, the gigantic bonfire took shape as the drum beat urged them on to work together in unison.

As the afternoon wore on, more people from the community arrived from the surrounding area and the usually quiet vineyard transformed into a vibrant, bustling festival ground.

In contrast to the vineyard workers in their practical, earth-toned clothing, local women swirled past in flowing skirts of emerald green and deep purple adorned with intricate floral embroidery. Men wore shirts of crimson and gold, and children darted between the adults wearing wreaths of wildflowers, their faces flushed with excitement. Many of the community had woven vine leaves in their hair and painted their faces with swirls of black charcoal and lines of clay in shades of ochre, reflecting their status as creatures of the land.

The air was alive with laughter and snatches of conversation in the lilting Somerset dialect. Rebecca caught fragments about crops and weather, and local gossip interspersed with phrases that sounded almost like incantations.

Near the edge of the field where the bonfire stood, a group set up a makeshift stage constructed from rough-hewn planks.

Five musicians climbed onto the platform, tuning up their unusual instruments. The fiddle was adorned with delicate chains of tiny bones that rattled with each movement.

The drummer's kit was decorated with antlers, creating an eerie forest of points above the skins. Even the guitar was strange, its body carved with intricate symbolic knotwork. The musicians were just as unusual as their instruments, wearing tattered black hoods that cast their faces in deep shadow as they practiced before the main event.

As the bonfire began to burn, a procession formed near it. People lined up, each holding something in their hands, as they approached the fire one by one.

Rebecca recognised Pam from the village shop, her expression sorrowful as she held out a faded photograph with trembling hands. She kissed it once, tears glistening on her cheeks, before tossing it into the flames. The fire flared briefly, consuming her offering.

A young couple held hands around a small, crude doll made of twisted straw. They both kissed it before throwing it into the bonfire.

One by one, the procession continued.

Letters yellowed with age, locks of hair tied with ribbon, small carved figures, all consigned to the flames. Each offering made the fire burn brighter. The flames took on strange hues of green, blue, and scarlet, and as one offering flared in the light, Rebecca thought she saw the face of the Green Man flicker before fading away.

She felt a little left out. There was nothing she needed to throw on the fire, but something made her want to join in and be part of the community. Just as her blood had mingled with the stag's, she wanted her offering to be part of the bonfire.

She hurried to the edge of the field and picked up some willow twigs, binding them with ivy stems and leaves into a circular pattern. She looped some wildflower stems, making three different shapes, to represent the phases of the moon.

Only when she had finished did Rebecca realise she had made something similar to Grace's carved pendant featuring the triple moon symbol, representing the maiden, mother, and crone. Perhaps it could be both an offering and a prayer, reminding her of why she had come to Somerset in the first place.

Rebecca joined the line and when she reached the flames, she whispered to whatever gods might be listening of her renewed desire to find out what happened to Grace, and asked for a blessing on her time at the vineyard. It wasn't much, but it made her feel more a part of the celebration.

She stepped back from the fire, her heart pounding as music swelled around her, and the scent of roasting meat and herbs filled the air.

As the last of the offerings were consumed by the flames, a hush fell over the gathering.

Rebecca turned to see Isabelle standing atop a small hillock, her silver hair glinting in the fading sunlight. The older woman raised her arms, and the crowd fell silent.

"The fire has accepted our offerings." Isabelle's voice carried across the field. "Now, we dance!"

A cheer went up from the crowd as Isabelle began to move, her body arching and dipping as she led the procession. Rebecca found herself caught up in the flow, swept along in a sea of colourful revellers.

They moved away from the bonfire, winding through the vineyard into an adjoining field as the procession took on a rhythmic quality, their feet stamping in time with the drums. Rebecca felt the beat in her bones, and her body swayed almost of its own accord.

As they crested a small rise, her breath caught in her throat.

An ancient maypole stood in the field, its weathered wood rising high into the twilight. Unlike the cheerful, ribbon-bedecked poles she'd seen at summer fairs, this one was roughly carved, almost primal, befitting a symbol of more dominant male fertility. It was woven with dark ivy and crow feathers, black roses and deadly nightshade.

When she reached it, Isabelle laid her hand on its gnarled surface. "Our community has used this pole for generations. It is our anchor to the earth, and our conduit to the sky. Tonight, we dance to awaken its power."

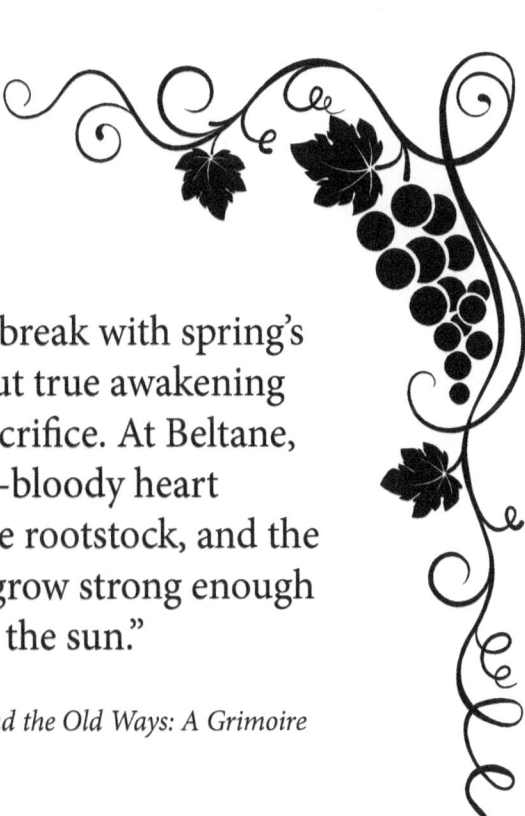

"The buds break with spring's warmth, but true awakening requires sacrifice. At Beltane, bury a still-bloody heart beneath the rootstock, and the vines will grow strong enough to strangle the sun."

—*Viticulture and the Old Ways: A Grimoire*

CHAPTER 15

Isabelle's words unleashed the crowd, and from seemingly nowhere, long ribbons appeared and were passed through the crowd, each person grasping one. Rebecca found a deep green ribbon pressed into her hand. Its texture was odd, almost organic, as if it was woven from the fabric of the land.

The band struck up a tune, the fiddle almost wailing as the drums beat once more, and over them, a pipe trilled with an eerie melody.

The dance began.

It started slowly as people wove in and out, and the ribbons began to wind around the pole. But as the music built, so did the frenzy of the dance.

Rebecca found herself caught up in the whirl, her feet moving as her heart raced, her breath coming in gasps.

In and out, under and over, again and again. The dancers wove a complex pattern around the pole as the ribbons created an ever-tightening web.

Rebecca caught glimpses of familiar faces in the crowd. Helen, her eyes wide with wonder. Liam, his usual reticence replaced by a wild abandon, and Nate, moving with a fluid grace that belied his gruff demeanour.

As they danced, Rebecca felt a change come over her.

She was no longer an outsider, a city girl playing at country life. She was part of an ancient tradition that ran generations deep.

The dance reached a fever pitch, the maypole now a patchwork of dark colours — deep green, midnight blue, dark crimson — overlaid with each other as the ribbons wound tighter and tighter.

Just when Rebecca thought she might collapse from the intensity, the music abruptly stopped.

Isabelle's voice rang out across the gathering. "The pole is tethered. The earth is awakened. Now, we feast and make merry, for tonight, all boundaries fall away!"

A shout of triumph went up from the crowd and Rebecca called out along with them.

A tap on her shoulder made her spin around.

"Thirsty?" Ben's face was flushed from the dance, and he held out a rough earthenware cup full of amber liquid. "It's local cider, just what we need after that."

Rebecca reached for the cup, her fingers brushing against Ben's as she took it. The touch sent a jolt through her, and their hands lingered, neither quite ready to break the contact.

"Thank you," Rebecca managed, her voice husky from exertion and perhaps something more.

She raised the cup to her lips and tasted it. Somerset was renowned for its cider, and this was sweeter than she expected, with an underlying complexity that hinted at ancient orchards and secret fermentation techniques.

"Hungry?" Ben asked, his words suggesting layers of meaning.

Rebecca nodded as she touched his chest with a flat hand, feeling his heartbeat. Whatever was building between them, it seemed as inevitable as the turning of the season.

They made their way back across the field towards the feast.

The scent of roasting meat grew stronger, mingled with

the sweet smoke of apple wood. A massive spit with a whole hog turned slowly over glowing coals, its skin crackling and glistening in the firelight. They joined the queue, the heat from the fire warming their faces as they waited.

When it was their turn, one of the workers handed them each a wooden trencher piled high with succulent pork, crisp crackling, and roasted vegetables that glistened with herb-infused oil.

They settled on a low stone wall at the edge of the festivities, enjoying the rich, fatty pork and the crunch of crackling.

Ben topped up their cider from a nearby barrel and raised his cup. "To Beltane."

"To Beltane," Rebecca echoed, clinking her cup against his. This batch of cider was stronger, its sweetness undercut by a sharp, almost bitter note.

As they drank, the long blast of a horn rang out. Its low, sonorous note reverberated through the night air, causing an immediate hush to fall over the crowd.

A single drum began to beat, its rhythm slow and deliberate.

The scattered community moved closer, forming a wide circle around the bonfire as the flames danced higher, casting long, twisting shadows across the ground.

From the darkness beyond the firelight, they emerged.

At first, Rebecca thought they were a flock of enormous birds, their movements fluid and unsettling. But as they drew closer, she realised they were Border Morris dancers, unlike any she had seen before.

Gone were the white clothes and bright colours of traditional Morris dancers. These dancers wore garments of deepest black, tattered and torn, as if they had clawed their way up from the grave.

Dark feathers sewn into the fabric rustled with each movement, and there were more feathers — crow, raven, and others Rebecca couldn't identify — entwined in their hair, along with black flowers that seemed to consume the firelight.

Smears of charcoal surrounded their eyes, an echo of the full blackface once traditionally worn. In the flickering light, the dark pigment seemed to shift and move over their skin.

"The Night Gathering," Ben whispered. "A local side. Apparently they only perform on nights like this, when the veil is thin."

They formed a circle, moving with an otherworldly grace, as if the ancient spirits of the land had taken physical form, rising from the earth to dance once more.

A fiddle joined the drum, its melody eerie and discordant. The dancers began to move, raising blackthorn sticks still covered with thorns high above their heads.

The clack of wood on wood rang out, sharp and violent, as the dancers wove in and out of complex patterns, their sticks a blur of motion as they hit against each other in an ancient rhythm.

"They say the dance is a battle," Ben murmured, his lips close to her ear. "A fight to keep the dark forces at bay for another year."

Rebecca shivered, leaning into him. "And if they lose?"

"Then we all pay the price."

The drum beat faster, becoming frenzied as the dancers matched its pace.

Their movements became wilder, more abandoned. Feathers flew from their costumes, edged with bright flame from the bonfire as they spiralled into the night air.

One dancer broke from the circle and stalked towards the crowd, his tattered cloak raised like feathered wings.

The nearest revellers gasped and stepped away, but Rebecca found herself rooted to the spot. The dancer's gaze locked onto hers, and in its depths, she glimpsed something primitive and hungry.

For a moment, the world fell away and Rebecca was

elsewhere — in a time long past, or perhaps yet to come. She saw the land beneath her, wild and untamed. Blood seeped into the earth, as screams of ecstasy and agony intertwined around her. The vines of Standing Stone writhed like tentacles, reaching, grasping. Consuming. They ruled this land. They always did, and always will, merely tolerating the humans who lived but a brief span upon their back.

The dancer whirled away, rejoining the circle.

The vision faded.

But as the ragged group spun ever faster, Rebecca glimpsed something beneath the figure's tattered clothes — not skin, but bark, gnarled and twisted like the ancient vines.

The dance reached its climax in a blur, spinning faster than should be possible, the music a cacophony that drove them on.

With a final, thunderous clap of their sticks, it was over.

Silence fell, broken only by their ragged breathing and the crackle of the bonfire.

The dancers stood motionless.

Then, as one, they turned and walked back into the darkness beyond the firelight.

No applause followed them, only a collective exhale from the crowd, as if everyone had been holding their breath.

There was a beat of silence, a pause between the acts of night.

The fiddle started up again, this time a joyous reel, and the atmosphere shifted.

Couples danced in the open space before the bonfire. The band struck up again and more people joined in until it seemed like the entire field was full of dancing and laughter, and the sheer delight at being alive.

Ben stood up and stretched out his hand. "Dance with me?"

Rebecca took his hand, feeling his rough calluses against her palm. As he pulled her to her feet, the world seemed to tilt. Whether from the cider or the night's strange energy, she couldn't tell.

They joined the whirling crowd, the fiddle's melody weaving through the air as the beat of the drum pulsed through the earth, up through Rebecca's bare feet and into her core.

She could smell wood smoke and sweat, the sweet ferment of spilled cider, and beneath it all, the rich, dark scent of freshly turned soil.

Ben's arm circled her waist, pulling her close, and they moved together, finding a rhythm as old as the land.

All around them, other couples danced with wild abandon. Rebecca caught glimpses of flushed faces, eyes bright with firelight and desire, as hands roamed freely, grasping at fabric and flesh alike. Laughter and snatches of song came from the shadows at the edges of the field, punctuated by gasps and low moans of pleasure.

As she spun with Ben, Rebecca tipped her head back. The stars wheeled overhead, so bright here, away from the city. For a dizzying moment, she felt as if she might fall upward into the vast, glittering expanse.

As the music slowed, their dance grew more intimate.

Rebecca was acutely aware of every point of contact between them — his hand on the small of her back, his thigh pressed against hers, his breath warm on her neck. The rest of the world faded away, leaving only the two of them in a bubble of firelight and music.

She leaned in. Their lips met, and a spark ignited between them.

The kiss deepened, became urgent, more desperate. Rebecca tangled her fingers in Ben's hair. He tasted of cider and smoke and something wild and untamed.

All she had to do was give herself to it and walk with him into the shadows. Together they would join with each other and the earth.

The music edged towards darkness, the melody twisting into something ancient and primal, urging them on.

Rebecca pulled away, meaning to lead Ben away from the crowd.

But as she took his hand, the flames of the bonfire leaped higher, casting twisted shadows across the ground.

Amongst the community of dancers, she glimpsed ragged dancers, their silhouettes flickering as if formed of smoke. They moved with inhuman grace, entwining themselves with those lost in the dance, as if to become one with their flesh.

One figure turned.

Rebecca gasped as she saw its horns and felt its gaze upon her.

"Rebecca?" Ben's voice came from far away. "Are you alright?"

She blinked and shook her head, forcing a smile. "I'm fine. Just... overwhelmed, I guess. It's a lot to take in."

Ben's answering smile was warm and reassuring. "It can be intense, your first Beltane. Do you want to get some air? Maybe we could go for a walk in the vineyard?"

The invitation was clear, but Rebecca hesitated, torn between desire and a sense of unease. The vineyard beckoned beyond, dark and inviting, promising pleasure in its hidden depths.

She certainly wanted Ben, and her body ached for his touch. But she couldn't shake the feeling that once she stepped into those shadows, something else might take hold of her — of them.

She stepped away from Ben, breaking their contact. "Actually, I'm feeling a bit heady. That cider must have been stronger than I expected. I'll just sit out the next dance, and I'll call it a night soon. But you carry on." She pointed into the whirling mass of dancers, people she recognised from the community and others from around the region who celebrated together. "This is too much fun for you to miss."

Ben hesitated, his gaze darting out to the crowd and back to her. "I can sit with you if you like. Make sure you get back to your bunk safely."

She shook her head. "No, seriously, you stay. I'm fine. Enjoy yourself."

He took her hand once more and kissed the back of it. "If you're sure, then. See you tomorrow. Hopefully without a killer hangover."

As Ben whirled into the crowd, Rebecca made her way to the edge of the field and leaned against a gnarled oak, breathing more easily now she was away from the wild centre of the celebration.

The bonfire still blazed, casting long shadows across the revellers who danced and laughed around it.

Perhaps Ben would end up in the vineyard with someone else tonight. Perhaps she had missed her chance.

But the horned figure had rattled her, coming as it did after the strange vision. Was there something more in the cider or in the herbs on the food that changed her perception? Maybe she just needed to go to sleep.

As Rebecca turned to walk back to the bunkhouse, she noticed Liam standing on the edge of the field, half-hidden in the shadows. The flickering firelight played across his face, his gaze fixed on a couple dancing intimately as their hands explored each other.

The intensity of Liam's stare was unsettling, as if he were both attracted to the couple and repulsed by the dance of fertility before him.

He must have felt her gaze and turned to glance over.

Rebecca quickly looked away, not wanting him to know she'd been watching, and headed for the bunkhouse.

CHAPTER 16

LIAM WATCHED AS REBECCA stumbled away from the Beltane celebration, her steps unsteady in the dim light. The bonfire's glow faded behind her, leaving her silhouette wavering against the darkness of the vineyard.

He frowned, wondering why she was now alone. She'd been dancing with Ben earlier, their bodies entwined in a way that made Liam's chest tighten with the memory of loss. But now she was alone, clearly affected by the night's revelry.

With a quick glance back at the dancers to make sure no one was watching, Liam made a decision. He'd make sure she got back to the bunkhouse safely. Follow her at a distance and she wouldn't even know, but at least she'd be safe. The rural night was full of predators, and tonight, there were more than ever.

It was the right thing to do. The Christian thing, a voice whispered in the back of his mind, and he pushed it away with a grimace.

He kept to the shadows at the edge of the vineyard rows as he followed her, feeling the weight of the night press down upon him. The Beltane celebration, with its rituals and uninhibited dancing, stirred forbidden urges deep within — urges he'd tried to bury. But the energy of the pagan festival had awakened them once more, and with the effects of the cider and whatever herbs were in it, he struggled to keep them from breaking forth.

As the vines whispered around him, their young leaves rustling in a breeze he couldn't feel, Liam thought of the parish he'd left behind.

The young teacher's face flashed before him, her eyes wide with hurt and betrayal. He had thought they shared something special, something pure. But she accused him of abusing his position of power and claimed she had not given consent. The church dismissed him, and now he wandered, with no idea where he might land next.

He was still so angry and, to be honest, he was confused at how the generations seemed to be so different. Young people now had such strange ideas about permission, ideas that certainly had no basis in the Bible. How was anyone meant to find a partner when the rules were so unclear?

Ahead of him, Rebecca swayed slightly and reached out a hand to steady herself against a gnarled vine.

Liam couldn't help looking at the curve of her hip, the graceful line of her neck, and he felt a familiar heat rise within. Ben had warmed her up, so she would be in need of some attention. He wondered what it would feel like to—

He took a step towards Rebecca, and something hanging from the vines brushed against his face.

He drew back, startled, and swiped at his face with agitation. It must be a spider web or something.

But as he looked again, he saw a length of knotted vine, adorned with feathers and daubs of what looked like blood. There were pieces of bone attached by stems of flowers, giving the whole thing a sense of a pagan charm.

There was a god here at Standing Stone, but not the god Liam once knew. This one lived in the soil and the vines, and it was older even than the god he used to serve. This one demanded the base part of human nature, made of blood and bone and animal desire — that which lay beneath the civilised self. Perhaps this god was more to his taste, after all.

Rebecca was almost at the bunkhouse. Liam needed to reach her before she stepped inside, as there were probably others within.

He pushed aside the dark charm and stepped onto the path with light footsteps so she wouldn't hear him.

A sound drifted through the night air.

A low moan of pleasure from somewhere deep within the vines, then a cry of ecstasy.

The surrounding vineyard was alive with passion, as couples sought release, emboldened by the festival, and Liam stood rooted to the spot, torn between his desire to pursue Rebecca and an overwhelming urge to watch whatever was happening in the shadows.

After a moment, he stepped into the vines and followed the sounds of pleasure from those who had surrendered to the wild call of Beltane.

Liam crept into the spirals of the labyrinth, using the curtains of leaves and the long grasses to hide his approach.

He caught sight of bare limbs entwined as the sounds of pleasure grew louder.

He moved so he could see more of the couple.

It was Nate, his muscular body thrusting into a young woman, her hair interlaced with flowers.

Her head was tipped back in ecstasy as Nate gripped her neck with one hand, holding her down to the soil of the vineyard beneath. It was violent, primal, but the young woman writhed in clearly consensual pleasure, an offering to the god of this land.

Her fingernails raked down Nate's back, drawing beads of blood, and he laughed as he pushed into her harder, faster.

The young woman wrapped her legs around Nate's hips, urging him deeper, and as Liam leaned in to see more closely, he stumbled against the vines.

The couple paused mid-thrust, looking toward the sound but showing no sign of embarrassment.

"Come closer," the young woman called out. "Join us. All are welcome at Beltane."

Liam's heart beat faster as he stepped out of the vines, the stir of desire overtaking him.

Nate smiled in welcome as he thrust again into the young woman, nodding as he did so at a jug. "Drink that and join us. Tonight we give our pleasure to fertilise the land."

Liam downed the rest of the cider in the jug as he stripped off and joined the couple on the hard earth. The sensations of touch and taste seemed enhanced by the drink and Liam gasped as the woman reached for him, losing himself in her.

The vineyard was alive around them as tendrils moved with an unnatural, serpentine grace. They swayed and curled in the night air, the vine tips reaching out to caress the lovers' skin as the leaves rustled with a sound like whispered incantations, an ancient language long forgotten by human ears.

The vines wound around them, binding them to each other, binding them to the earth, and the sensation on his skin took Liam to a new level of pleasure.

As he thrust into the young woman beneath him, he felt Nate's firm hands close around his throat.

At first, he welcomed the man's touch, which urged him to greater intensity.

Shadows danced at the periphery of Liam's vision, twisting and writhing in the air in a mimicry of the lovers. But these shadows were old and wild — and hungry.

A tendril of vine brushed against Liam's cheek as it wound itself around Nate's hand and began to tighten. It wrapped more loops and contracted in pulses like a serpent.

Liam bucked and writhed, grasping at his neck in desperation as he fought for breath.

But more vines wrapped around his wrists, pulling his arms apart.

Beneath him, the young woman wrapped her legs around

his hips and held him tight. Her pupils were wide, her lips parted with pleasure and dark fascination as Liam thrashed in pleasure and pain, unable to escape the tightening grip.

Images flashed before his eyes.

An ancient rite performed in a forest glade before even the Romans walked this land. Blood seeping into eager soil, as ecstatic dancers merged with each other and the land itself. He saw the cycle of seasons stretching back millennia and felt the weight of countless harvests and sacrifices. The God he once believed in had no power here.

As his vision went dark and his breath caught one last time, Liam thought he glimpsed a horned figure amongst the vines.

CHAPTER 17

THE MORNING SUN STREAMED through the bunk-house windows, waking Rebecca from fitful sleep.

Her head throbbed with the aftermath of the celebration, and she groaned softly as she sat up and ran a hand through her tangled hair.

The events of Beltane felt distant and hazy now, like a half-remembered dream. The pulsing rhythm of the drums, the whirling dancers with their crow-feather cloaks, the hungry eyes of the horned figure in the shadows. In the clear light of day, it all seemed far-fetched, and Rebecca wondered what kind of herbs might explain her fevered imagination. Helen would know.

Rebecca glanced over to the older woman's bunk, but Helen was still and deeply asleep. That could wait until later. For now, she desperately needed coffee and fresh air.

Dressing quickly, she made her way outside and squinted against the brightness of the early morning sun. The vine-yard looked peaceful in the early light, with bedraggled ribbons the only evidence of the celebration. The other fields must need a lot more clean-up, no doubt the focus of the community today.

As she walked towards the kitchen for coffee, movement across the yard caught Rebecca's attention.

Nate emerged from the butchery shed, his muscular arms straining as he pushed a large, heavy wheelbarrow with a tarpaulin covering its contents. It must be a big animal for Nate to struggle so much with it.

She instinctively stepped into the shadow of the nearest building and watched as Nate headed to the restricted area of ancient vines, turning a corner to unlock and enter the hidden side gate. Rebecca followed at a distance, staying out of sight but desperate to see inside, even briefly.

As he pushed through, she had a glimpse of what lay inside.

The vines looked different from the carefully tended rows of the main vineyard. They were wild, untamed, with leaves of deepest green glinting with an almost metallic sheen, and the fruit was heavy, with an imperial purple lustre. It was way too early for the grapes to be so ripe, and the rest of the vineyard had no fruit at all. Was there something in this location and the direction of the sun that made it mature so much faster — or was there something different in the soil?

Nate shut the gate behind him, blocking off her view.

As she headed into the kitchen, Rebecca wondered if she could find out anything more from the library. The wild layout and the different colours inside sparked an idea for enhancing a wing of the new buildings, and she needed to know more about that area. Perhaps if she showed Isabelle an expanded design, she might even be allowed inside the gates for a closer look.

Once everyone was up, much later than the usual start time, the vineyard workers and others from the community pitched in to clean up the aftermath of the festival.

The fields were a sprawling mess of trampled grass, discarded cups and wooden plates, and the detritus of cel-ebration. Several of Rebecca's fellow workers were already there, muddling through the work with the slow, careful movements of the thoroughly hungover. She caught sight of Ben across the field, his hair wild and unkempt. Their eyes met briefly, and he smiled warmly in greeting. Rebecca felt a twinge of regret at what might have been last night, but the long summer was still ahead, so perhaps there would be another chance.

The massive bonfire was now just a wide circle of ash and charred logs, wisps of smoke still rising from its depths. A couple of workers raked the embers, spreading them out to help them cool more quickly. In the ashes, there were edges of bone and metal, remnants of the ritual offerings.

"Rebecca!" Isabelle called out as she clambered up the rise. "Come and help with the maypole."

Rebecca headed up and over, joining Isabelle and five others in the adjacent field. The ancient pole loomed overhead, its dark wood seeming to draw in and consume the sunlight. The ribbons wrapped around it, intertwined with dark ivy and black roses, now hung limp and faded, like tattered banners in the aftermath of battle.

Together, the team worked to topple the pole and lay it gently on the meadow ground, before slowly cutting away everything on its surface.

As Rebecca worked her section, she uncovered intricate carvings along the pole. They had been hidden last night, but now she could see they reflected aspects of the ancient celebration.

Human figures contorted into impossible positions as they danced, or made love amongst the vines. Animals—some recognisable, others nightmarishly mutated—wound their way through the vines that crawled across the surface of the pole. Their tendrils, some tipped with sharp thorns, reached out as if to ensnare whatever they touched.

At the top of the pole was a face, neither human nor animal, but something in between. Its eyes were hollow, its mouth open as if to devour a sacrifice. Horns sprouted from its forehead, curling back like crescent moons over a wild tangle of what might have been hair or leaves, evoking a twisted version of the Green Man.

"Quite something, isn't it?"

Rebecca started at the sound of Isabelle's voice beside her. She hadn't heard her approach.

"It's… unusual," she managed, unable to take her eyes off the carving.

"The maypole has been in the community for generations, and some say it's as old as the vineyard itself. We enact some of its stories every year at Beltane." Isabelle turned to Rebecca, her gaze intense. "Did you enjoy last night? Did you feel part of the community?"

Her questions felt like another test, and Rebecca took a beat before she answered.

"It was strange and wonderful, all at the same time. The music and the dancers, well, I think I heard the call of the vines then."

Isabelle smiled broadly and reached out to squeeze Rebecca's hand. "Oh, I'm so pleased. You really fit in well here. I'm looking forward to seeing the next round of your architectural drawings, especially as you are bound to the land now. We might even get planning permission before the harvest."

Another worker shouted from across the field, and Isabelle headed off to help, while Rebecca walked back through the bonfire area to help pull down the band's stage.

It looked like everyone was there now, but then she realised she couldn't see Liam. She recalled his intense stare during the Beltane celebrations, the way his eyes had burned with some inner conflict.

Nate was dismantling part of the stage, kneeling over a section of wooden flooring that had been unscrewed but still needed to be lifted and stacked away. He grunted as he shifted one of the heavy boards, trying to balance it against his knee, but it was awkward work, the kind that was easier with two pairs of hands. He glanced up, scanning the field for someone to help. He waved at Rebecca.

"Can you help me with this?"

Rebecca hurried over and crouched down beside him, her fingers brushing against the rough edges of the wood. Together, they lifted the panel, the weight of it pressing into their palms, and moved it to the side where they stacked it against the wall.

As they worked, Rebecca glanced over at Nate. "Have you seen Liam today? I think he might have had too much cider last night. I haven't seen him this morning."

Nate straightened from his work, letting out a breath as he wiped his brow with the back of his hand, a smear of dust streaking across his forehead. "Liam decided to leave Standing Stone, I'm afraid. He said Beltane was a step too far."

Rebecca frowned. "He left? Just like that, in the middle of the night?"

"I took him to the village early this morning, before most people were up." Nate shrugged. "Some folks just aren't cut out for life here, and you know he used to be a Christian minister, right? The old ways, the connection to the land — it can all be overwhelming for those who are not open to it. The vineyard only calls to some." He gave her a searching look. "Does it call to you, Rebecca?"

A cloud passed over the sky, casting them both into shadow, and Nate's gaze darkened.

Rebecca nodded. "Sometimes, if I open my mind enough. That cider certainly helped."

They laughed together, and the shadow of the cloud passed on.

As Nate turned to help some others with the base of the stage, Rebecca thought back to seeing him early this morning, and wondered when he could have had time to take Liam into the village.

She pushed her questions aside, focusing instead on the warmth of Nate's approval and Isabelle's kind words. She had found acceptance here and an openness to new ideas she had never found back in London. The community had even begun to take the place in her heart that her parents and sister had left bare.

There was something special here, something real and vital, and whatever had spooked Liam, she was made of sterner stuff. She would see this through, no matter what.

CHAPTER 18

June arrived at Standing Stone Cellars with a flourish of warmth and vibrant life. The Somerset countryside burst into full bloom, painting the landscape with a palette of green and gold and rainbow hues. Early morning mist gave way to clear azure skies, and the sun's golden rays encouraged an abundance of growth.

In the vineyard, the once-bare vines now boasted lush canopies of emerald leaves. Tiny flower clusters emerged, their delicate petals unfurling to reveal miniature, star-shaped blossoms. The air hummed with the gentle buzz of bees drawn by the sweet fragrance of the grape flowers.

Rebecca loved the variance of her days. Research in the library allowed her architectural mind to run wild, and manual labour in the vine rows balanced it with physical movement. Both were interspersed by the office hours needed to transfer her designs to electronic format and to wade through local council planning forms.

One afternoon, she went to help Helen in the poly tunnels, long, curved shelters covered in thick, translucent sheets of plastic that bathed everything in soft, diffused light. Warm and humid, the air inside smelled of earthy soil and the fresh, green fragrance of new growth, mingling with a faint tang of sun-warmed plastic.

Rows of vegetables and herbs lined the beds, each plant thriving under the protective canopy that trapped heat and held off the chill, allowing for a longer growing season. Tomato vines wound their way up slender strings, their glossy leaves brushing against Rebecca's arms as she passed, next to clusters of tender lettuce, spiky fennel fronds, and aromatic basil.

Rebecca enjoyed her time with Helen, as the older woman's enthusiasm was infectious and she shared her botanical knowledge freely. Together, they tended to the vegetables and herbs that supplied the vineyard's kitchens and contributed to its biodynamic preparations.

"It's all about balance," Helen explained as they worked side by side, the rich soil dark beneath their fingernails. "Every plant has a purpose, a role to play in the grand design of the vineyard, and biodynamic principles honour this."

Rebecca nodded as she harvested some salad leaves. "It's fascinating how interconnected everything is. I never realised how much thought went into every aspect of wine production until I came here."

"Oh, it goes far beyond just the wine. We cultivate an entire ecosystem here. Every plant, each insect, every micro-organism in the soil — they all work together in harmony."

As they worked, Rebecca opened up to Helen, sharing her ideas for the vineyard's future. The older woman listened attentively, offering insights and suggestions that added depth to Rebecca's concepts.

"I love how you're thinking about integrating the new structures with the landscape," Helen said as they paused for a water break. "Have you considered incorporating some of these companion plants into the buildings themselves? Living walls, perhaps, or rooftop gardens?"

Her words sparked a cascade of other ideas, and Rebecca couldn't help her enthusiasm spilling over. "That's brilliant. We could create vertical gardens that are both aesthetic and functional. It's much better for water management as well. Imagine a tasting room surrounded by walls of flowering herbs, the scents mingling with the bouquet of the wine. It would be wonderful."

Helen nodded. "And it would provide natural insulation, helping regulate temperature inside the buildings. Eco-friendly and cost-effective." She brushed some soil off her hands. "Right, that's enough in here for now. Come and help me with the planting beds around the southern perimeter."

They walked out together and worked methodically side by side, creating a living barrier of flowers and herbs designed to attract beneficial insects and deter pests. Lavender lined the pathways with purple flowers swaying gently in the breeze and marigolds added splashes of vibrant orange and yellow, their pungent scent a natural deterrent to harmful creatures, as nasturtiums sprawled in cheerful tangles, their bright flowers a favourite of pollinating insects.

"We'll put some more chamomile here." Helen pointed to a sunny spot near the edge of a vine row. "It's excellent for attracting hover-flies, which prey on aphids. And over there, we'll plant yarrow, a powerhouse of a plant. It attracts predatory wasps, provides habitat for ladybirds, and its deep roots help break up compacted soil, as well as being used in the biodynamic preparations."

Rebecca absorbed every word, her imagination racing as thought of ways to incorporate more such beds into her expansion designs. She envisioned winding paths bordered by beneficial plants, creating not just functional barriers but a new sensory experience for visitors.

"What are these?" She gestured to a group of plants with delicate, star-shaped leaves.

"Borage." Helen smiled. "One of my favourites. The flowers are a magnet for bees, and they're edible, too. Lovely in salads or as a garnish for summer drinks. And see how the leaves are slightly fuzzy? That texture deters some pests."

Helen gestured to a more secluded corner of the vineyard, almost the farthest point from the manor house. "Let's have a look over there. I know Nate likes to keep that section wild, but I want to check that the biodiversity is managed well enough. We don't want it overrun with bindweed."

The section was wilder, less manicured than the orderly rows of vines they usually worked among. Tall grasses swayed in the gentle breeze, and wildflowers dotted the landscape with splashes of vibrant colour.

Helen moved through the area with light steps and the grace of someone intimately familiar with the land. Her keen eyes scanned the ground, cataloguing the various plants they encountered, identifying the species, and explaining their properties and uses.

Suddenly, Helen stopped, her brow furrowing in concern. "Oh my," she murmured and crouched down to examine a cluster of plants with purple, hood-shaped flowers.

"What is it?" Rebecca asked, hunkering down beside her.

"Monkshood," Helen replied, her voice tight. "And over there, that's deadly nightshade." She pointed to a plant with bell-shaped flowers and shiny black berries. "Both highly toxic. They can cause paralysis if ingested. We can't risk anyone accidentally coming into contact with these."

She pulled on her gardening gloves and began carefully uprooting the monkshood, taking care not to touch any part of the plant with her bare skin.

As they worked, Helen identified more potentially harmful plants in the area. "Over there, that's hemlock. Oh, and henbane too." She shook her head, a worried frown creasing her forehead. "It's odd that so many poisonous plants should grow here. It's not wild at all. This has to be deliberately cultivated."

"I've heard of henbane," Rebecca said, recalling snippets of information from her research. "Isn't it used in some traditional practices?"

Helen nodded. "Yes, it has hallucinogenic properties, but it's also incredibly dangerous if mishandled." She redoubled her efforts, pulling up the plants with increasing urgency. "I can't believe how many toxic species grow here. We need to clear them out before someone gets hurt."

They had amassed a decent pile of uprooted plants when a shout rang out across the field. "Stop! What the hell do you think you're doing?"

Rebecca looked up to see Nate running towards them, his expression contorted with anger. He reached them in seconds and roughly shoved Helen away from the pile.

"Have you lost your mind?" he snarled, eyes blazing. "These are sacred. How dare you uproot them!"

Helen stumbled back, her face pale. "They're dangerous. They could poison someone—"

"Poison?" Nate spat the word out like a curse. "You don't understand anything. These plants are crucial to the balance of the terroir. The wine needs bitter as well as sweet."

Rebecca tried to intervene. "Nate, we were just trying to make it safer—"

Nate rounded on her, his gaze so intense that she took an involuntary step back. "You don't know enough. Perhaps you never will. But Helen" — he turned to the older woman — "should know better."

Helen's lower lip trembled, and she burst into tears. "I'm sorry, Nate. I didn't realise—"

"No, you didn't." Nate bent down and began gathering the uprooted plants, handling them with a reverence that contrasted with his harsh words. "Get back to the greenhouse. Leave the wild plants alone. You're not to come to this area again, do you understand?"

Helen nodded mutely, tears streaming down her face. She turned and hurried away, her shoulders shaking with suppressed sobs.

Rebecca watched her go, torn between following her

friend and staying to help clean up the mess. She turned to Nate, who was carefully gathering the plants.

"I'm sorry, and I know Helen is, too. We didn't mean any harm. She was just worried about safety."

Nate sighed, his anger dissipating now Helen was gone. "I know you meant well, but you have to understand—everything here serves a purpose. Even the plants you might consider dangerous or toxic. They're part of the balance we've worked so hard to achieve. The land needs them to feed the soil, to grow the vines, to keep our community alive."

Rebecca nodded. "Why are these in particular so important?"

"The roots of these plants run deep, intertwining with those of the vines. They absorb minerals from the soil, changing its composition in subtle ways. When they decay, they return those minerals, along with their own unique properties, back to the earth."

Nate pointed to the monkshood. "This, for instance. Its alkaloids seep into the soil, creating a slight bitterness that adds complexity to our wine. And the nightshade contributes to the deep, almost smoky notes in some of our reds."

Rebecca was fascinated, despite her lingering concern. "And the henbane? The hallucinogenic properties?"

Nate smiled, his gaze lingering on the plant with a hint of longing in his eyes. "Ah, that's special. It doesn't directly affect the grapes, but it's crucial for some of our traditional practices. Rituals that have been performed here for generations. That connect us to the land. As you experienced at Beltane."

Rebecca remembered her visions from that night and thought of the darker batch of cider. A touch of henbane would certainly explain a few things.

Nate stood, carefully cradling the uprooted plants in his arms. "I'm going to replant these now. In the future, if you have concerns about any of the plants you find, come to me first. Don't take matters into your own hands."

Rebecca nodded. "Of course. I'm sorry again."

He smiled, the last of his anger fading. "It's alright. You're still learning. That's what matters."

Rebecca made her way down the hill, her mind churning with the day's events. She couldn't shake the image of Helen's tear-stained face or the fierce protectiveness in Nate's eyes as he gathered the uprooted plants.

The memory of Beltane flickered through her mind — the intoxicating cider, the vivid hallucinations, the way the air had seemed alive with ancient power. What other rituals might go on here that required such potent, dangerous ingredients?

Helen sat in the shade of an oak tree and imagined her body sinking into the solid trunk, where she might not feel the wound of Nate's words. She had stumbled down the hill away from the wild area, her vision blurred by tears, finding solace here in the quiet. She felt humiliated, her years of experience and good intentions crushed by Nate's harsh words.

But sitting here wouldn't solve anything. Perhaps she could go and see Isabelle and explain what had happened. Maybe Nate was in the wrong, after all.

She wiped her tears and walked back towards the communal bathrooms to wash her face. It would be puffy from crying.

As she passed the administration building, she heard a voice call out. "Helen? Are you okay?"

Helen turned to see Asha, her expression etched with concern.

"Oh, it's nothing, dear. Just a little misunderstanding, I'm sure."

Asha gently took Helen's arm and guided her into the marketing office. "Come on, I could use your help with something. It'll take your mind off whatever it is."

Helen allowed herself to be led, grateful for the distraction.

The marketing area was all sleek lines and modern technology — a stark contrast to the organic shapes of the vineyard.

Asha sat Helen down in front of a large computer screen and pulled up some designs.

"I'm working on invitations for an upcoming exclusive event. I'd love your input on the floral elements to make sure they are true to what grows here."

As Asha clicked through various layouts, Helen found herself drawn in. The designs were extraordinary, blending traditional vineyard imagery with modern, almost abstract interpretations of local flora. "These are beautiful. You're very talented."

Asha beamed at the praise. "Thank you! I want them to capture the essence of Standing Stone, you know? The tradition, but also the unique elements that will attract those who want a different kind of vineyard experience."

They discussed different flower choices and colour schemes, and Asha took meticulous notes with an ornate Montblanc pen. Helen noticed several photos pinned next to the computer: Asha with an older couple, presumably her parents, and some younger children who must be her siblings. They all shared Asha's warm smile.

A sharp pang of longing almost made Helen gasp. She'd never been blessed with children of her own, a fact that had haunted her for years. After her husband died, she had no one, and seeing Asha's family photos, evidence of the young woman's connections and roots, made Helen acutely aware of her own isolation.

"Your family looks lovely," Helen whispered.

Asha glanced at the photos and smiled. "They are. I miss them, but it's nice to have a reminder nearby."

As they continued working, Helen found her mind wandering.

Why exactly had she come to Standing Stone? The promise of sustainable, biodynamic practices had drawn her, for sure, and she had hoped to contribute her botanical knowledge to a worthy cause.

But increasingly, she felt out of place.

The vineyard's methods, while intriguing, often veered into territory that made her uncomfortable. And now, after Nate's outburst...

"Maybe I don't belong here after all," Helen muttered.

Asha looked up, surprised. "What do you mean? Of course you belong here. Your knowledge is invaluable."

Helen patted Asha's hand, touched by the young woman's kindness. "Thank you, dear. I just... I'm not sure I understand this place as well as I thought I did."

Later that evening, Helen made her way to the dining hall, her earlier altercation with Nate still weighing heavily on her mind. Just as she was about to enter, she felt a hand on her shoulder.

"Helen, wait." It was Nate, his expression contrite. "I wanted to apologise for earlier. I'm sorry, I shouldn't have shouted like that. It was an overreaction."

Helen nodded stiffly, not quite ready to forgive.

Nate held out a glass of deep red wine. "Peace offering? It's from our reserve stock — the better stuff." He winked. "Don't tell the others!"

After a moment's hesitation, Helen accepted the glass and his apology. "Okay, I'm sorry again, and thanks for this."

Throughout dinner, Helen sipped the wine, feeling its warmth spread through her. It was indeed delicious, definitely a different vintage than the wine normally served to workers. But by the time the meal ended, she felt distinctly woozy and her vision blurred at the edges.

She stood, swaying slightly.

Isabelle appeared at her elbow. "Are you alright, Helen? You look a bit peaky."

Helen shook her head, trying to clear it. "I'm fine, just… perhaps a bit too much wine."

"Come with me," Isabelle said. "You can use my private bathroom. It's more comfortable than the communal ones."

Helen nodded gratefully, allowing Isabelle to guide her around to the manor house.

The opulent bathroom was a blur of marble and gleaming fixtures. Helen barely registered that the door didn't lock as she stumbled to the toilet, her stomach clenching.

As she leaned over the bowl and vomited violently, a horrible realisation dawned.

The symptoms were familiar.

Too familiar.

Flashes of the toxic plants she'd uprooted earlier raced through her mind. Could they have been in her food? In the wine?

Fear gripped her as the edges of her vision darkened.

Helen tried to call out, but her voice was weak, barely a whisper. "Help… please…"

As her consciousness faltered, she lay down on the floor, anchoring herself to the cool tiles even as the weight of her body seemed to float away.

The door opened.

Through her rapidly narrowing vision, Helen saw Isabelle enter. The vineyard owner sat beside her and stroked Helen's hair with tenderness and a kind smile.

"Shh, it's alright, now," Isabelle murmured. "You can rest. The plants will be well cared for after you're gone. We'll bury you under the poisonous plants, and your body will nurture their growth. As it must be."

Helen tried to speak, to scream, but her body wouldn't respond.

As darkness closed in, the last thing she saw was Isabelle's serene smile, touched by something that might have been regret — or perhaps anticipation.

CHAPTER 19

SUNLIGHT FILTERED THROUGH THE thin curtains of the bunkhouse, casting a warm glow over the room. Rebecca stirred awake, blinking as she oriented herself, and turned to look at Helen's bunk. She hadn't seen the older woman after dinner when she'd left with Isabelle.

The bunk was empty, and the sheets and blanket neatly made. Rebecca frowned, a sense of unease settling in her stomach. It wasn't like Helen to be up and about so early — if anything, she'd expected her to want more rest after yesterday's upset with Nate.

Perhaps she had simply risen early to tend to the greenhouse, throwing herself into work as a distraction. Or maybe she'd gone for a walk to clear her head. Still, Rebecca couldn't shake the feeling that something was off.

As she made her way up to the library, the vineyard was already alive with activity. Workers moved between the rows of vines, their voices an indistinct murmur in the morning air.

Rebecca entered the manor house, the old wooden floors creaking beneath her feet. The scent of freshly brewed coffee led her to the kitchen, where she found Isabelle standing at the counter, a steaming mug in front of her.

"Morning!" Isabelle raised her mug. "Coffee's just made. Help yourself."

Rebecca filled a mug with the bitter black and took a sip. "Have you seen Helen today? She wasn't in her bunk this morning. I wanted to check if she was okay, as she had a falling out with Nate yesterday."

Isabelle sighed as she leaned against the counter. "She wasn't feeling well, probably from the stress of the disagreement. She came up here, and we talked late into the night. The incident with Nate affected her deeply, so she decided to leave. I got one of the local workers to take her into the village."

Rebecca frowned. "But she loved it here. Her work in the greenhouse, the border planting. She was so passionate about it all, and I saw Nate apologise last night."

"Indeed, but when people realise that a place isn't the right fit for them, it's best if they leave. Best for them. Best for us." Isabelle took another sip of her coffee. "Helen didn't understand the deeper aspects of what we do here. Not like you. You've taken to everything beautifully. Your understanding of the land, your vision for the expansion. You're exactly what Standing Stone needs."

Rebecca felt a mix of emotions swirling within her. Disappointment at Helen's departure and concern for her friend's well-being, but also a warmth at Isabelle's words. Unlike Helen, she fitted in. She was needed.

"Thank you. That means a lot. I'm excited to continue working on the plans. Speaking of which, I should probably get to the library."

Isabelle nodded. "Of course. Don't let me keep you. And don't worry too much about Helen. I'm sure she'll be fine once she's back home, away from all this." She waved her hand vaguely, encompassing the vineyard and all its mysteries.

As Rebecca left the kitchen, she couldn't help but feel a twinge of guilt at how quickly her concern for Helen had faded in the face of Isabelle's approval, especially since the older woman had given her some great ideas for vertical gardens.

But then, Helen had chosen to leave, and as Isabelle said, the older woman hadn't really fitted in.

Up in the library, Rebecca settled at the mahogany desk. She spread out her sketches and notes and added additional details, incorporating some ideas sparked by Helen's comments.

As she worked, Rebecca kept thinking of something she'd read in one of the older books. It had mentioned ley lines, ancient pathways of energy that crisscrossed the land. Perhaps they were part of the terroir, too, and perhaps she could incorporate them into the design.

She set aside her current sketch and began pulling books from the shelves, paging through different tomes as she lost herself in earth energy, sacred geometry, and the power of place.

Hours slipped by unnoticed as she pieced together a fascinating picture.

According to ancient maps, the Standing Stone vineyard lay at the convergence of powerful ley lines, and the nexus point lay within the restricted area. Rebecca considered how she might use this to convince Isabelle to let her inside those gates. After all, how could she design something coherent without seeing every inch of the land?

She sketched out new ideas, using the ley lines as a guide, and barely noticed the morning slipping into the afternoon.

Eventually, her alarm went off, breaking her concentration. Time for her afternoon shift in the vineyard.

She headed out deep into the labyrinth rows, the once-bare vines now transformed into lush corridors of green, their leaves a tapestry of emerald and jade stretching to the horizon.

Rebecca moved down the rows, her now-practiced hands adjusting leaves and checking for signs of disease or pest damage. The heady scent of sun-warmed earth and foliage rose, and bees buzzed amongst the vines, their drone a contented background hum punctuated by bird song.

A gust of wind suddenly rustled through the vines, and Rebecca looked up, noticing for the first time the dark clouds gathering on the horizon. A storm was rolling in and the sky to the west was now a turbulent mass of slate grey and deep purple.

"Looks like we're in for some weather," a familiar voice called out.

Rebecca turned to see Ben approaching, a warm smile on his face despite the darkening sky.

"I didn't even notice it coming," Rebecca admitted, returning his smile. "I guess I was too caught up in the vines."

Ben nodded, understanding in his eyes. "They have a way of doing that, don't they? Drawing you in until the rest of the world fades away. Here, I'll help you finish the row before the storm comes."

They continued together, working in comfortable tandem. Ben's firm hands moved with practiced ease among the vines and Rebecca couldn't help but remember how his fingers had felt on her skin.

The wind picked up, bringing with it the first spatters of rain as the temperature dropped. Fat droplets fell sporadically at first, then with increasing frequency.

"We should head in," Ben said, over the growing patter of rain on leaves.

But Rebecca felt rooted to the spot, exhilarated by the storm's energy. "We're already wet. We might as well stay."

Ben grinned, and they continued to work, moving faster now, almost dancing between the vines as they raced to finish the row before the storm grew too intense.

The rain fell harder, soaking through their clothes. Rebecca's hair clung to her face in wet tendrils, and rivulets of water ran down her arms as she reached to adjust the canopy of a particularly tall vine. She felt alive, her every sense heightened by the storm's wild energy and the smell of wet earth and the verdant green land.

Lightning flashed in the distance, followed by a low rumble of thunder.

The wind whipped through the vineyard, causing the vines to sway and dance.

At the end of the row, Ben turned to Rebecca, his eyes bright, his face flushed.

For a moment, they simply stood there, rain streaming down their faces.

Then, as if moved by the force that drove the storm, they came together.

Ben's lips met hers, and Rebecca felt as though electricity coursed through her veins, channelled from the sky, through his mouth and into the earth. She pressed herself against him, and their kiss deepened, becoming more urgent.

Rebecca tangled her fingers in his wet hair, while his hands slipped under her T-shirt onto her bare skin, pulling her closer.

They were lost in each other, oblivious to the raging storm, its wild energy flowing through their intertwined bodies.

The scent of petrichor — rain on dry earth — mingled with the heady aroma of ripening grapes as they sank to the ground, the wet soil cool against Rebecca's back. The vines swayed above them, and she imagined their leaves brushing her skin like a thousand gentle caresses, even as Ben explored her body with his rough hands.

Lightning flashed again, illuminating Ben's face above her.

In that moment, Rebecca saw in his eyes a reflection of the primal force that pulsed through the vineyard. Thunder rolled overhead, its deep rumble resonating in her chest, matching the rhythm of her pounding heart.

As they moved together, Rebecca felt the boundary between her body and the earth dissolve. She could sense the intricate network of roots beneath her, the slow, steady heartbeat of the ancient vines, and she was part of it all.

The rain washed over them, each drop falling as it had since the dawn of time, and their joining was just as ancient, a celebration of life and growth and renewal.

When it was over, they lay together in the wet grasses and wildflowers under the vines, and listened to the storm gradually subside.

The rain softened to a gentle patter, and shafts of golden sunlight pierced through the breaking clouds. The vineyard glistened in the aftermath, every leaf transformed into a prism, scattering rainbow light.

"We better go get changed," Ben said softly. "We might be discovered if we lie here much longer."

Rebecca turned in his arms and kissed him once more, a slow, lingering touch that promised more. Her body ached in a deeply satisfying way, and she wondered when they might get a chance to do this again.

Ben was clearly thinking the same thing, for as they pulled their clothes on, he reached out a hand to caress her arm. "It's the summer solstice tomorrow. Will you meet me to watch the sunrise? There's a spot on the hill with an amazing view of the vineyard, and it's secluded enough that we could be alone."

Rebecca grinned. "I'd love to."

As they made their way back, hand in hand, Rebecca felt as though she was walking on air.

The vineyard had never looked more beautiful, and the vine leaves seemed to nod approvingly as they passed. This was what she had been searching for — a place where she belonged, work that fulfilled her, and now, someone she might share it with.

In that moment, she was truly happy.

They dropped each other's hands as they came into view of the bunkhouse, but then Ben spun Rebecca into the shadows of the vines for one last kiss.

"Until tomorrow," he murmured.

CHAPTER 20

REBECCA WOKE BEFORE HER early alarm, eager to see Ben. The bunkhouse was silent, her fellow workers still lost in dreams as she walked out into the pre-dawn darkness.

Outside, the world held its breath, poised on the edge of the longest day as Rebecca made her way to the end of the bunkhouse, the gravel crunching softly beneath her feet.

Ben was already there, a thermos in one hand and a backpack slung over his shoulder. He reached for her hand. "Morning. Fancy coffee on the hill... and maybe some dessert?"

Rebecca smiled at the promise of pleasure ahead. "Lead the way."

They set off and soon left the rows of the vineyard behind. The path wound uphill, becoming steeper and more over-grown as they climbed. Rebecca's breath came in short gasps, but the exertion felt good, grounding her in the moment.

As they neared the summit, the eastern sky lightened with a pale wash of colour. Ben reached back, offering his hand to help Rebecca over a tricky section. The warmth of his touch lingered even after they'd moved on, and she craved his touch on her skin once more.

Finally, they reached the top of the hill and turned to look at the view.

The vineyard spread out below them, a patchwork of green and gold in the growing light. Beyond it, the Somerset countryside rolled away to the horizon, a tapestry of fields and hedgerows.

"It's so beautiful here," Rebecca sighed. "I can't believe I thought my life in London was enough, when all this was only a few hours away."

Ben set down his backpack and pulled out a blanket. They sat close, shoulders and thighs touching as they sipped hot coffee from the thermos.

The sky continued to brighten, the colours shifting and changing with each passing moment.

Then, suddenly, the sun crested the horizon. Golden light spilled across the land, setting the world ablaze.

Rebecca gasped, overwhelmed by natural beauty. In that moment, she felt completely connected to the land, to the turning of the seasons and the ancient rhythms that pulsed beneath the surface of modern life.

"Happy solstice." Ben gently turned her face towards him as he leaned down and brushed his lips against hers.

Their kiss deepened, and Rebecca reached for him.

Electricity sparked between them, but Ben groaned and pulled away. "I'm sorry, I want you so badly, but there's something I need to tell you before we take this any further. I should have told you earlier. Before yesterday."

Rebecca turned to face him, a mix of curiosity and apprehension flooding through her. "What is it?"

Ben took a deep breath. "You won't tell anyone?"

"Of course not."

He sighed. "I'm still working for the vineyard I told you about in France. They sent me here to find out how the hell Standing Stone produces their award-winning wines. They are too good, almost impossible for this climate, and biodynamic methods alone can't explain it."

Rebecca reeled back at his words. "So you're... what?

Spying on them? Trying to steal their secrets?"

Ben winced at her words. "I prefer to think of it as research, but yes, I suppose that's what I'm doing." He took her hands, his expression earnest. "I've found some strange things that go way beyond what's normal for a vineyard, even a biodynamic one."

He looked around furtively, his voice dropping to a near whisper despite their isolated location. "The preparation shed has all kinds of weird concoctions in it, some definitely not part of biodynamic recipes, and there's this mural on one wall, hidden behind some crates. Figures dancing among the vines, and a horned creature, and what looked like a sacrifice."

His words brought back Rebecca's experience on her first day in the preparation shed, when she had seen the mural, along with visions in the dynamiser, and heard the song of the vineyard.

"And that's not all," Ben continued. "I've heard sounds at night coming from the restricted area of the vineyard. Chanting, as well as screams and moans, maybe pain, maybe pleasure, and I've seen Nate go in there with something large and dead, wrapped in a tarpaulin. Surely you've noticed that not everything is normal here?"

Rebecca's head spun as she considered his words. It was indeed strange here, but surely that was just part of rural life, and the richness of the terroir and the award-winning wine came from the unique blend of it all.

The practices here were old and perhaps not entirely conventional, but perhaps they could be explained as a unique blend of pagan practice and modern biodynamics. She'd certainly found evidence of that in some of the older books in the library.

But then she thought of the disturbing mural, the wild Beltane celebration, and the horned shadows dancing at the edge of her vision.

"I don't know what to think," Rebecca admitted. "Some days I question what I might have seen, and I am disturbed by some practices. But other days I feel deeply connected to something special here. An energy in the land that calls to me, and a community who has welcomed me in."

Ben nodded. "I can see how much you love it here, and that's part of why I'm telling you this now. Your designs for the expansion, your understanding of the land — it's incredible, and I know Isabelle and Nate see your promise. But I'm worried what might be asked of you if you become too deeply involved."

Rebecca pulled her hands away from his. "I'm already deeply involved. Isabelle has approved my designs and we're moving to the next stage — planning applications, costings, timelines. This is more than a job for me now."

Ben sighed and ran a hand through his hair. "That's why I need your help. Isabelle trusts you, and you have access to the house and the library."

Rebecca frowned. "You want me to spy on her for you? I can't do that."

"I know it's a lot to ask," Ben said, his voice pleading. "But think about it. If there is something sinister going on here, don't we have a responsibility to uncover it?"

Rebecca stood and walked to the edge of the hill, needing to put some physical distance between them.

As she gazed out over the vineyard, the neat rows of vines now fully illuminated by the morning sun, everything looked beautiful and peaceful. How could something so lovely harbour anything sinister?

She wanted to reject Ben's request, to stay in the safety of unknowing, but his words caused doubts she had pushed deep down to resurface.

She had originally come here to look for Grace, and somehow she had been coaxed from her path by the promise of a new life at Standing Stone.

The vineyard had become more of a home than she'd ever expected, and Isabelle showed great trust, offering her a chance to make a real impact with her designs.

The community here had welcomed her, and Rebecca felt like she belonged here in a way she never had in London. But if there were indeed dark secrets here at Standing Stone, might they be connected to her sister's disappearance? Was this the chance she'd been waiting for to finally uncover the truth?

"I need to think about it," she said finally. "This is a lot to take in."

Ben nodded and stood to join her. "I understand. Just, please promise me you'll keep this a secret? If Isabelle or Nate found out, I'm not sure what might happen."

Rebecca remembered Nate's violent outburst at Helen, and his muscular arms straining as he pushed a heavy wheelbarrow into the restricted area. As much as she respected the man, she didn't want to get on his bad side.

"I won't say anything, but that doesn't mean I'll help you."

He nodded. "Of course. Just be careful, okay? And remember, I'm here if you need me."

He leaned in to kiss her again, but Rebecca pulled away.

His words had chilled any desire and soured the possibility of anything they could have had together. As much as her body wanted more of his, she couldn't stop her conflicted thoughts.

She needed time to think.

They began the trek back down the hill, the mood between them markedly different from their excited climb in the pre-dawn darkness, and the distance between them growing wider with every step.

CHAPTER 21

WHILE REBECCA LOVED BEING out in the verdant abundance of the vineyard, learning new skills and old ways of working with the vines, she still felt most at home in the library. Every day, she grew more confident that her new designs would both honour the vineyard and help the business flourish even more. Keeping busy also meant she could avoid Ben and the conflicting thoughts she still struggled with.

The enormous mahogany desk was now covered with her drawings and plans for the vineyard, and reference books were piled within easy reach of her chair. Isabelle occasionally came to check on the developments, but most of the time, Rebecca was alone.

She could hear the sounds of vineyard workers outside and the cheerful birdsong from the nearby trees. The background noise kept her company, and she was content to work for hours there.

Isabelle had approved several iterations of the plans already, but Rebecca still wanted to learn more about the older aspects of the land that made up the vineyard. It had changed hands many times over the years, always with a female owner, and its prosperity had waxed and waned, as all endeavours must. But the ancient part, fenced off and kept exclusive, was much larger than Rebecca had expected, at least according to some of the older maps, and she hadn't made it through the oldest archives in the library yet. She was determined to finish going through them today.

She wheeled over the library ladder and placed it against the bookcase with the oldest volumes. There were some near the top she wanted to examine more closely.

Rebecca climbed the stairs and reached up for the first book, her fingers brushing against the spines of those on the shelf next to it. One of spines felt different, like soft textured leather. It was too far up to see clearly, so she stood on tiptoe and reached even further.

The ladder wobbled, held.

She pulled out the book and climbed back down to the safety of the library floor.

Her heartbeat quickened as she recognised the book as the one she had seen briefly on Isabelle's desk that first day at Standing Stone. *Viticulture and the Old Ways: A Grimoire.*

It had clearly been placed out of easy reach, but Isabelle had never expressly forbidden her to access anything in the library, and she encouraged Rebecca to learn the old ways, so surely it was okay to have a closer look?

The weight in her stomach told her no — this book was not for her eyes, not yet. Even holding it in her hands felt like a transgression.

But the urge to look was too strong.

Rebecca laid it on the desk on top of her plans and opened the leather-bound cover.

A wave of scent rose from its pages. The rich aroma of freshly turned soil, the acid of fermenting grapes, the musty sweetness of autumn leaves. For a moment, Rebecca felt as if she stood in the heart of the vineyard rather than the library — and then she caught the metallic tang of blood as an after note.

She turned the first few pages to get a sense of the book.

The paper was thick and yellowed, the text written in an elegant, spidery hand. There were intricate illustrations of the vines at different times of the year and images of flowers and other plants. Interspersed between the vines were pagan sigils and horned creatures.

There was also a warning:

"Only those who feel the beat of the vineyard in their blood, and those who hear the call of the vines, may safely wield the power herein. To all others, beware. The Horned God will take his due from the transgressor."

Rebecca shivered, despite the warm day. The threat was clear, and although her logical mind said she did not believe in these pagan superstitions, she had seen strange horned shadows, and at Beltane, she had indeed heard the call of the vineyard.

Part of her wanted to take the book back up the ladder and return it to its place and never think of it again.

But what if there were some revelations within that would help with the final stage of her design? Or perhaps some of the organic imagery would help deepen her plans?

She turned the page and began to read.

The first few chapters covered sigils of growth and protection, with intricate diagrams of symbols and where to place them in the vineyard, which explained the carvings on the end of the vine rows. There were lunar cycle charts and diagrams of hand-cranked machinery.

The next section covered the creation of potent, plant-infused preparations, tonics, and wines. Some were variations on the biodynamic versions Rebecca had already learned with Nate, but then there were pages which encouraged a darker use.

There were draughts for seeing visions that used wormwood, henbane, and belladonna — some of the plants Helen had pulled out before she'd left the vineyard.

"Harvest under the dark of the new moon, steeping them

in the year's first pressing for a full lunar cycle. The resulting elixir will open the mind to the whispers of the vine and the secrets of the earth."

Rebecca's breath caught. This confirmed her suspicions that the elixir had been in the dark batch of cider at Beltane.

She read on. There were recipes for dealing with pests and for speeding decomposition of dead animals, so that their body parts could be returned to the earth more quickly. Detailed illustrations showed animal corpses splayed open, with notations indicating how different organs could fertilise specific areas of the vineyard. There were instructions for communing with the spirit of the vine and divining the future in fermentation tanks.

Rebecca came to the last section of the book, marked by an illustration of a skull with crescent moon horns surrounded by an abundance of vine leaves and grapes. She found herself transfixed by the pitted eye sockets of what must be the Horned God. The same creature that was carved on the community's ancient maypole.

She reached out with a fingertip to turn the page.

A sound from outside the library startled her from her reverie.

Footsteps, slow and deliberate, along the corridor.

Quickly, Rebecca closed the grimoire and slipped it under some of the plans, her heart pounding as she pretended to focus on her architectural diagrams.

The footsteps paused outside the library.

After a beat, whoever it was walked on.

Once the sound had faded down the stairs and her heart rate had slowed down, Rebecca let out a shaky breath. She pulled out the grimoire and once more turned the page.

The next section was titled "Summoning the Horned God of the Vine." Intricate diagrams covered the pages, showing a circular arrangement of standing stones with a central altar, and text describing a ritual to be performed when the veil to the next world was thin.

"The chosen vessel is tied to the altar. As the knife pierces flesh and blood flows onto the stone, call to the Horned God. Let the life force of the sacrifice seep into the earth and feed the roots of the ancient vines. Only then may He be called forth to walk among us and bless the harvest for another year."

While there was no image of the blood sacrifice, it was clearly no symbolic ceremony, and presumably these were the standing stones beyond the stave gates. Could such rituals still be carried out there in modern times?

Her hands were shaking a little as Rebecca turned the final pages.

They outlined binding rituals for tying workers to the land, ensuring their loyalty to the vineyard. Some rituals involved contracts signed in blood, given willingly or not. Others called for burying personal items belonging to workers at specific points in the vineyard. The most disturbing rituals hinted at a form of human grafting, binding the worker's life force directly to the vines.

"Once bound, the servant — and those they love — belong to the vineyard. They shall know no rest, in this life or the next, until the last vine withers and the final grape rots on the vine. The bond can only be broken by finding another who accepts its yoke, willing or unwilling."

There were lists on the last few pages, long columns of names, all women, stretching back over centuries.

Rebecca scanned the list, recognising some names from local history books she had already been through. These were the women who had owned the vineyard over generations.

She paged through to the last name.

Isabelle, as expected, and then pages of blank space, waiting for the next custodians.

A sudden gust of wind rattled the library windows, making Rebecca jump.

The lamp on her desk flickered, causing the shadows in the room to dance and shift into the silhouette of a horned figure.

She blinked, and the figure was gone. But the sense of being watched, of some ancient and hungry presence lurking just out of sight, remained.

With trembling hands, Rebecca closed the grimoire. She climbed the ladder and placed it back on the shelf.

Her thoughts whirled as she considered all she'd read. This was exactly the kind of thing Ben was looking for, but could she tell him about it without jeopardising her place here?

This architectural project was the chance to fulfil her career dreams of designing a beautiful space with organic lines that was also functional and commercially viable. It could lead to so many more opportunities. She couldn't give it up.

The grimoire was just an old book of superstitions, and words on a page couldn't hurt her or Ben. She would keep quiet about it, at least for now.

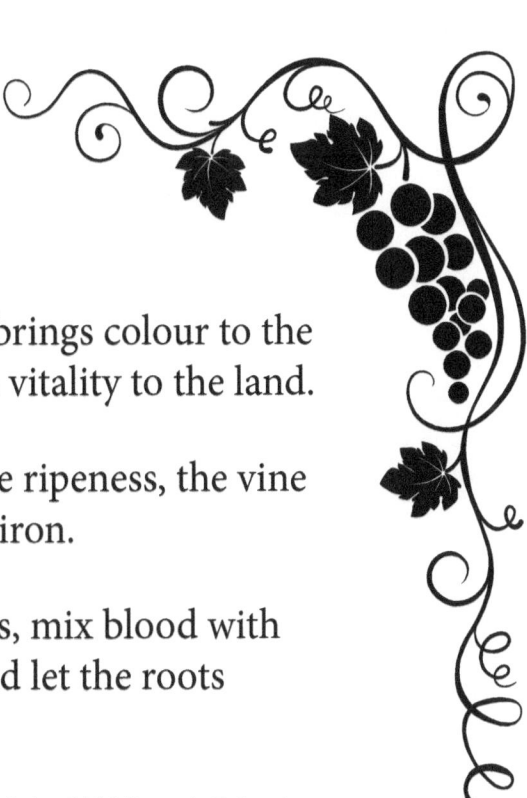

"Veraison brings colour to the grapes and vitality to the land.

But for true ripeness, the vine must taste iron.

At Lammas, mix blood with the soil, and let the roots drink."

—*Viticulture and the Old Ways: A Grimoire*

CHAPTER 22

THE SUMMER HEAT MADE the air shimmer above the vines as Rebecca walked through the rows. The vines were heavy with ripening grapes, clusters of tight, round berries hanging from their trellises, showing the first hints of deep purple, dusky blue, or pale green, depending on the variety. Leaves were full and vibrant, their broad surfaces soaking up the sunlight, occasionally curling at the edges from the heat of the season.

The air was thick with the sweet, slightly tangy scent of ripening fruit, mixed with the earthy undertones of warm soil. Bees and other pollinators buzzed lazily among the vines, drawn by the wildflowers between rows. Marigolds, nasturtiums, and clover thrived, adding bursts of orange, red, and green beneath the vines, serving both as natural pest deterrents and living mulch.

Rebecca paused at the entrance to the labyrinth section, and the memory of the rainstorm with Ben came flooding back. Part of her wished she could return to that moment and relive it, to capture the time before he told her of his true intentions at the vineyard.

She had been avoiding him for weeks now, making sure that her shifts didn't coincide with his, and merely nodding politely in the dinner hall. They had gone from lovers to distant acquaintances in such a short time, but Rebecca still wasn't ready to talk yet.

The transfer of her drawings and rough plans into the architectural AutoCAD software kept her busy in between long shifts in the vineyard, and the manual labour under the hot sun kept her occupied. Her skin had tanned, and she had become more muscular, and at night, she slept deeply from the day's exertion.

Rebecca had looked in the mirror this morning and wondered at her transformation from the pale, unhealthy woman she'd been in London. The vineyard had changed her life for the better in so many ways, and she didn't want Ben to threaten the new sense of home and purpose she'd found.

But she couldn't avoid him any longer as the vineyard and community celebrated Lammas today, also known as Lughnasadh. It was the beginning of the harvest season, and if Beltane was anything to go by, the celebration would be strange and wonderful all at once.

The sound of bells rang out in a peal of celebration, a sign for all workers to come in from the fields.

Rebecca headed into the courtyard to find it hung with garlands of wheat and woven wildflowers, and the scent of freshly baked bread made her stomach rumble.

Isabelle stood in the centre of the courtyard, directing the final preparations. A wreath of wheat and cornflowers crowned her silver hair, and she wore a flowing dress of duck egg blue that shimmered in the sunlight as she encouraged workers on with a smile.

Isabelle waved Rebecca over and gestured to a long wooden table where a group of women were gathered. "Come and join us!"

The table was covered in stalks of wheat, dried corn husks, and an array of colourful ribbons and threads. The older women worked fast, weaving and twisting the materials into various shapes as they whispered words of blessing.

"We're making corn dollies," Isabelle explained as she pointed Rebecca to an empty spot at the table. "It's an ancient tradition honouring the spirit of the harvest."

Rebecca sat down and picked up a few stalks of wheat, unsure about what to do with it. Some of the women created simple plaits, while others crafted more elaborate figures — harvest maidens with flowing hair made of corn silk, and fertility symbols with exaggerated curves.

Branwen sat at one end, her gnarled fingers twisting together strands of knotted wheat stalks and feathers to make a kind of witch's ladder. Next to her, another woman formed a horned creature from tangles of wheat and wild grasses.

"Lammas is a time of transformation," Isabelle said. "We stand at the threshold between summer and autumn, life and death. The grain gives itself so that we might live and, through our corn dollies, we symbolically echo the natural world."

One of the younger women leaned over to Rebecca. "Here. I'll show you how to start."

After the demonstration, Rebecca found herself lost in the work, growing more confident as she twisted and braided the wheat. She managed to make a simple braided loop tied with a ribbon by the time everyone else finished their more elaborate creations.

"Now, we move on to the Blessing Bread," Isabelle announced, passing around a large wooden bowl filled with a rich, yeasty dough. Each woman took a handful, kneading it gently before adding it back to the bowl.

"As you work the dough, focus on your hopes for the coming harvest. Pour your energy into the bread."

Rebecca closed her eyes as she kneaded, trying to clear her mind of doubts and focus on positive thoughts. The dough was warm and alive under her hands, and she found herself thinking of the vineyard, of the swelling grapes and the promise they held for the future.

When she opened her eyes, she saw Isabelle watching her intently, a look of approval on her face.

As the bread was set aside to rise, the courtyard filled with more people. Villagers arrived carrying baskets and crates, and set up makeshift market stalls around the sides.

Rebecca wandered amongst the stalls, taking in the vibrant display of local produce. Plump tomatoes glistened next to bunches of fragrant herbs. Jars of golden honey caught the sunlight, while wheels of cheese promised rich, complex flavours. It was a feast for the senses, a celebration of the nature's abundance.

Rebecca had occasionally gone to farmer's markets in London, but those urban streets were so far from the land where the produce was grown. Whereas here, Rebecca was beginning to understand the soil and the land in a more intimate and meaningful way.

As she circled around the courtyard, she found herself at the wine tasting booth.

Ben was there with some of the other workers, pouring samples for a group of enthusiastic visitors.

He looked up as she approached. "Would you like to try our new rosé?"

His voice was carefully neutral, but in his eyes, there was an entreaty. *Don't walk away.*

Rebecca nodded and accepted the glass he offered. Their fingers brushed as she took it and she brought the wine to her lips, tasting the fresh crisp sweetness.

She couldn't help smiling. "It's delicious."

Ben grinned. "It's from the south-facing slopes. You know, the ones near the oak tree with the barrel hive for wild bees? The grapes there get the most sun."

Rebecca took another sip, just as the music started up and a cheer rippled through the crowd. It wouldn't be a rural festival without some folk dancing, but the atmosphere was so different to Beltane. Rebecca couldn't imagine a side of dark Morris emerging in their cloaks and black feathers this time.

The music was joyful and light, and with the beat of the drum and the rattle of tambourines, couples began to dance, their feet moving in intricate patterns as children skipped and twirled at the edges of the circle, their laughter rising above the music.

"Would you like to dance?" Ben asked suddenly, setting down the wine bottle.

Rebecca hesitated, torn between caution and the desire to recapture some of the easy companionship they'd once shared. "I don't know the steps."

"Neither do I, but we can figure it out together."

He reached out a hand, and after a moment's consideration, Rebecca took it.

They joined the circle, awkwardly at first, but soon finding their rhythm. As they moved together, Rebecca felt some of the tension between them ease.

"I've missed you," Ben whispered softly, his hand warms on her waist.

"I've missed you too," Rebecca admitted. "But I'm still not sure what to think about everything you told me."

Ben nodded, his expression serious. "I know, and you don't need to do anything. I just want you to be careful."

As the music grew more riotous, the crowd continued to dance and drink as the sun sank lower in the sky. Dusk fell, and the courtyard was bathed in a soft, golden light. Lanterns flickered to life around the edges of the celebration.

As Ben spun Rebecca round, she caught sight of Isabelle at the edge of the gathering. She was gesturing to Nate and a few other key vineyard workers, her expression dark despite the joyous atmosphere as they headed off together into the shadows.

The hairs prickled on the back of Rebecca's neck and she tightened her grip on Ben's hand. "Don't stop dancing, but spin us closer to the manor house."

Ben raised an eyebrow, but he smoothly guided their steps in that direction, weaving through the celebrating crowd.

As they neared the manor house, Rebecca watched Isabelle lead the small group around the corner, their movements purposeful.

She pulled Ben into the shadows after them, staying well back but keeping them in sight.

Isabelle stopped on the side of the manor house closest to the most ancient part of the vineyard, where vegetation almost completely obscured a section of the wall. Thick tendrils of ivy snaked across the ancient stones, intertwined with thorny stems of black roses, their petals absorbing what little light remained. Isabelle bent down and opened a latch. Nate helped her to haul open a heavy door, its well-oiled hinges making no sound.

Rebecca's breath caught in her throat. She knew the layout of the manor house from her work on the expansion plans, and this door had to lead to that mysterious room connected to the wine cellar.

The small group entered. The heavy door swung shut behind them with a dull thud, followed by the click of a lock.

"Let's take a closer look," Ben whispered.

Rebecca hesitated a moment, but she needed to see what that door might be. Those within surely wouldn't emerge too soon, so it was the best chance they had to explore.

They hurried over with light footsteps and, in the dim light, examined the door more closely. The ancient wood seemed to pulse beneath Rebecca's fingertips as she traced the intricate symbols carved on its surface, along with the shapes of vine leaves and grapes.

The grooves of the unfamiliar runes felt warm, almost

alive, as if they held the imprints of countless hands that had touched them over centuries. Each symbol whispered a language just beyond her comprehension, hinting at forgotten knowledge and forbidden rites Rebecca could never learn from books in the library. They had to be experienced in person.

A horned creature nestled amongst the carved vines, its features both human and bestial. Its eyes glinted with malevolent intelligence, and its mouth twisted in a leering grin that spoke of primal urges and eternal hunger. It was the same figure from the mural in the preparation shed.

Ben leaned in close, his breath warm on her neck as he studied the carving. "You've seen that figure before, right? The Horned God. It's an ancient figure representing the untamed aspects of nature. Fertility, the wild hunt, the cycle of life and death. He demands sacrifice in exchange for a good harvest."

The sound of rhythmic chanting started beyond the door, the words indistinct but almost hypnotic. Underneath it all came a low, pulsing beat that Rebecca could feel in her bones, as if the earth beneath them awakened. The crawling ivy around the walls seemed to move towards the sound, and in their branches, Rebecca noticed shapes of ancient faces contorted in silent screams.

Whatever this was, it was not meant to be witnessed. They couldn't be discovered here.

As she pulled Ben away, Rebecca thought she saw the carved vines writhing on the door, and the Horned God turn its head to watch them go.

CHAPTER 23

REBECCA WALKED AROUND THE curve of the labyrinthine block of vines, examining the heavy bunches of fruit.

Each cluster of grapes hung low, their skins taut and glossy, catching the pale autumn light in a way that made them seem to glow from within. The once-vibrant green of summer had softened to rich hues of burgundy, indigo, and the occasional golden bunch, as though the sun had chosen some for its own. The surrounding leaves, still clinging to the last vestiges of green, rustled softly in the breeze.

As she worked, Rebecca considered how much this place had wound itself deep within her, and even the more unusual aspects of Standing Stone seemed just part of the unique mix of elements that made up the terroir.

Soon these grapes would be picked and turned into wine that others would drink. In it, they would taste a fraction of the land's bounty, and perhaps in that mouthful of bliss find escape, even just for a moment. Then the cycle would start all over again — and there was something deeply reassuring in that.

Millenia had passed since the Romans ruled this land but even back then, the annual cycle of the vineyard was the same — and, with biodynamic practices, perhaps even the day-to-day operations were not so dissimilar. Rebecca walked in the footsteps of those who had worked the land for generations, which made her feel even more a part of the community.

She thought of the mysterious room in the wine cellar and the disturbing carved doors that led to it, the grimoire with its description of sacrifice, and, of course, the restricted area of the vineyard. She was desperate to know more, and hopefully to dispel the doubts that she and Ben had about Standing Stone.

But Rebecca resisted further investigation on their own. It was too risky.

Perhaps, if she could become a more useful member of the community, and if Isabelle trusted her enough, she would be invited inside and learn everything she needed to set her mind at ease. Ben's suspicions and her own intuition had intensified into doubt and uncertainty, but she would risk her place here if she were discovered. Indulging her curiosity just wasn't worth it right now.

The architectural plans were in good shape and proceeded through the council's planning permission process. If approved, they could begin preliminary work next year, with Rebecca overseeing it all. She smiled as she considered what that project would mean to her, after too long working on projects designed for utility, not beauty, and destroying nature rather than enhancing it. She was a long way from London now, in every way.

Voices came from below on the hill.

Rebecca turned to see Nate and Isabelle walking up through the vines, checking the bunches of grapes as they went.

Isabelle waved. "Come down. You can help us decide whether it's time for harvest."

Rebecca joined them and together they examined a few bunches.

"I think we're ready, but let's double-check." Nate pulled

an almanac from his back pocket, its burgundy cover marked with the year. He flipped it open to a page covered in colourful bar charts and cryptic symbols.

"This is the biodynamic calendar. It's how we time everything in the vineyard, and luckily, there's enough of a community worldwide that a central company publishes these. Many here are experts in natural cycles, but these charts make decisions easier."

Rebecca leaned in to examine them more closely. "What do all these colours mean?"

Nate ran a calloused finger along the page. "Each represents a distinct part of the plant — fruit, flower, leaf, root. See how they change day by day? That's the moon and planets influencing which part of the plant is most receptive."

Rebecca pointed to the strange glyphs in the rightmost column. "And these symbols?"

"They're constellations," Isabelle explained. "The moon's position affects the energies flowing through the vineyard. We have to work with that energy, not against it. Just as the moon pulls the tides and tugs at the moisture in the vine sap, it stirs the blood within us all."

She reached out and gently caressed a leaf. "Like us humans, plants are mostly water. When the moon is waxing, it pulls that water upward, energising the leaves and fruit. During the waning phase, that energy retreats into the roots. We're as much at the moon's mercy as these grapes, and that ties us all together."

A gust of wind rustled through the leaves, and for a moment, Rebecca could have sworn she heard whispers on the breeze. Whispers that spoke of earth energy and lunar cycles and cosmic forces that had shaped life since the beginning of time.

Nate gestured back at the rows of vines. "We can honour this ancient wisdom and harness its energy, with some help from science." He held up the almanac. "According to this, we're approaching a fruit day. The moon will be in Sagittarius, a fire sign, which is perfect for harvesting. Fire signs amplify the energy in the fruit, bringing out the fullest flavours and vitality. This is when the grapes are at their most expressive, soaking up every bit of the sun's warmth and the earth's richness."

He traced his finger over the lunar cycle marked on the page. "We need to complete the harvest while the moon is descending. During this phase, the energy is concentrated in the fruit, not the leaves or stems, which means the grapes will be more flavourful and balanced. It's all about timing—capturing the moment when the vines are in harmony with the cosmos."

Rebecca nodded, considering what some might call superstition. Yet she had seen enough at Standing Stone to know that there was power in these ancient practices, and perhaps this was how they made the award-winning wines that Ben was so interested in.

"While we honour the cycles of the land, we're also a business." Isabelle pulled out a small handheld device from her bag. "We measure the Brix, the sugar levels, in a more scientific way. This is a refractometer. It measures how much light is bent, or refracted, as it passes through the juice, a direct indicator of the sugar concentration."

The device was compact, with a sleek metallic body and a textured grip designed for easy handling.

Isabelle flipped open the clear, protective cover to reveal a small glass plate.

Nate selected a grape from one bunch and carefully squeezed a drop of juice onto the plate. Isabelle closed the cover gently to ensure the juice spread evenly over the surface. She raised the device and peered through the lens, adjusting the focus to see more clearly.

"The scale inside shows us the Brix level," Nate explained. "It tells us the percentage of sugar by weight, which varies by grape variety. Higher Brix means riper grapes and more potential alcohol. For our Pinot, we aim for twenty to twenty-two Brix."

Isabelle lowered the device and smiled, clearly satisfied with the reading. She reached into the row and plucked a grape, inspecting it for a moment before putting it into her mouth and savouring it slowly, concentration in her expression.

"Numbers are important, but they're only part of the story. We have to taste the fruit. Feel the balance of sugar, acid, and tannin. The Brix level can tell us a lot, but it's the taste that truly reveals whether the grapes are ready."

She reached for another grape, rolling it between her fingers before biting down, her eyes closing as she concentrated on the flavours. "The flesh, the skins, even the seeds—they all tell us something. You can't get that from a number. It's about the moment the fruit speaks to you, when it tastes alive with the season's energy. Numbers don't make the wine—we do, with every taste, every touch. But you still have to understand the science."

She handed the refractometer to Rebecca. "Here, have a look."

Rebecca took it and looked into the device, adjusting it until the scale within came into sharp focus. The light passed through the juice, and a clear demarcation line appeared on the Brix scale. It was almost a relief to find evidence of scientific viticulture after the more esoteric practices at the vineyard.

"I didn't realize you relied much on science here," Rebecca said carefully, handing the device back to Nate.

"It's about finding the perfect balance where natural cycles and science meet, and where we get the best possible wine from what the land has given us." He gestured at the rows of vines stretched before them. "We need to take more samples. One reading is a good start, but to get an accurate sense of the vineyard's readiness for harvest, we need more. We can't just rely on one cluster from one spot."

They walked on further into the vineyard and Isabelle pointed out different areas. "Each has its own microclimate, with slight variations in sunlight, soil composition, and drainage. These factors affect how quickly or slowly the grapes ripen, so we sample from different blocks, and within each block, we check different vines and bunches to make sure we're getting a good mix." She looked intently at Rebecca. "If you stay with us, you will quickly learn what's important."

Nate selected another area, and they stopped to measure again. "It's a lot of work, but this is how we ensure that when we do harvest, the grapes are truly ready.

While Nate tested more grapes, Isabelle turned to Rebecca. "Tonight, the Full Hunter's Moon rises, and with it, an opportunity. I'd like you to join me and a few select others tonight for a very special harvest."

"Yes, of course, I'd love to. Who else will be there?"

"Not me, that's for sure," Nate said gruffly, as he continued sampling.

"It's women only," Isabelle explained. "Those who hear the call of the land gather to harvest by moonlight, but only when the cycles align, and the Full Hunter's Moon is an auspicious night indeed."

Rebecca felt a thrill of excitement mixed with a touch of apprehension. "I'd be honoured to join you."

Isabelle's smile widened. "Excellent. Meet us at the edge of the labyrinth block just before moonrise."

Later that night, Rebecca made her way through the darkened vineyard. The full moon hung low and heavy in the sky, bathing everything in an otherworldly silver glow. As she approached the labyrinth, a group of women gathered in a loose circle loomed out of the darkness. Their faces were shadowed, but she recognised Isabelle's silver hair shimmering in the moonlight.

Isabelle beckoned her to join, and as Rebecca stepped into the circle, she felt a change in the air, as if she'd crossed an invisible threshold.

The other women nodded in greeting, but remained in silence.

Isabelle raised her hands, commanding attention. "Sisters, tonight we gather under the Hunter's Moon, a time of transition as the cycle turns once more, and a period of gathering before the dark months ahead. As women, our cycles turn with the moon and our feminine power peaks under its light."

Branwen brought forward a large earthenware jug of wine and some simple cups. As she poured the dark liquid out, Isabelle spoke again.

"Let us share in the bounty of past harvests, infused with the sacred herbs of our land to give us strength for the work ahead."

The cups were passed around the circle.

When Rebecca received hers, she inhaled deeply. The wine's aroma was intoxicating, layered with herbal notes that made her head swim even before she took a sip. She thought of the recipes in the grimoire, and doubt rose up inside. Should she really drink this? What might it do to her?

Isabelle raised her cup. "To the harvest, and to each other."

"To the harvest, and to each other," the women echoed.

Rebecca pushed her doubts aside and joined the toast, appreciating the sense of community under the moon as they all drank.

She felt a warmth spread through her body, radiating out from her core as the wine both relaxed and energised her for the night ahead.

"Feel the earth beneath your feet, sisters," Isabelle continued. "Feel the pull of the moon above. Let us become conduits between sky and soil, vessels for the ancient power that flows through this land."

Rebecca could almost feel the cool earth through the soles of her feet, and sense the vast network of roots spreading out beneath the vineyard as the moon's light intensified above them.

Isabelle pointed down at a stack of wicker baskets made from local willow wood. "Now, we harvest. Let the vineyard guide you and choose only the ripest fruit."

The women walked out into the labyrinth of vines, spreading out but staying within earshot of one another. Rebecca found herself before a heavily laden vine, its grapes glistening in the moonlight. As she reached out to pluck the first cluster, Isabelle began to chant, and the others joined in.

It was a rhythmic melody with ancient words that echoed some of the other songs Rebecca had learned in the vineyard. As the women sang, she sensed the pulse of the land and the heartbeat of the vineyard joining their own.

After a few rounds, she joined in, her voice blending with the others as she harvested ripe fruit, placing each bunch gently into her wicker basket.

The boundaries between her body and the vineyard blurred as the chant evolved, becoming more complex, with words in an ancient language she didn't know but somehow understood on a primal level.

Rebecca felt connected not just to the land and the other women, but to a long line of ancestors stretching back into the mists of time. This ritual had been performed countless times before and would be performed countless times again as the moon rose over this land, in a cycle as old as humanity itself.

Time lost all meaning as the women worked together, moving deeper into the labyrinth rows. The moon tracked across the sky, its light shifting and changing, casting unfamiliar shadows with each passing hour. Rebecca's basket grew heavy with fruit, each grape a concentrated drop of moonlight and earth. When each basket was full, the women carried it to a vat before returning to harvest once more.

Eventually, Isabelle called out, signalling the end of the harvest.

The women gathered once more in a circle, and as Rebecca looked around at her fellow harvesters, she saw them truly for the first time. Their eyes were bright with wild energy, their skin flushed and gleaming with exertion, and Rebecca noticed that Branwen looked noticeably younger than she did in the day.

Isabelle stood in the centre of the circle, her silver hair a halo in the moonlight. "Sisters, we have done well. The vineyard has blessed us with its bounty."

One woman brought forward a large wooden bowl, roughly carved with wild vines.

Isabelle bent and scooped up a handful of earth as she held a bunch of ripe grapes in the other. "With this soil, we mark ourselves as children of the vineyard, bound to its cycles of growth and decay. With these grapes, we mark ourselves with the blood of the land, so it will accept our sacrifice."

She bent down and mashed the grapes together with the soil in the bowl, then stood and drew a line of the dark red paste across her forehead.

The other women stepped forward in turn to mark themselves.

When it was Rebecca's turn, she dipped her fingers in and then wiped them across her cheeks. Part of her wanted more, wanted to stain more of her skin with the mixture so she would be bound to this place and these people. Another part of her recognised she was under the influence of something darker here, and yet she craved it.

When the ritual was complete, Isabelle raised her arms to the moon. "Bless our sisterhood and bless this harvest. May we honour the land with this crop."

There was silence for a second as the other women bowed their heads.

Then Isabelle clapped her hands, and the atmosphere changed as the women lingered, talking and catching up with community gossip.

Isabelle walked over to Rebecca. "Did you enjoy tonight?"

Rebecca nodded. "Thank you. It was truly special."

Isabelle's smile was knowing, almost conspiratorial. "You're part of the land now. The vineyard has accepted you, and may show you more secrets if you bind yourself closer to it."

As she walked back towards the bunkhouse, Rebecca wondered what more she might learn as time passed — and what would she give to be part of it?

Tonight, she had been granted access to something powerful and primeval, but she knew that such power always came at a price.

CHAPTER 24

ASHA STOOD AT THE entrance to the manor house, smoothing down her figure-hugging black dress for what felt like the hundredth time. The air carried the scent of ripe grapes and wood smoke, a heady mix that only heightened her nervous excitement.

She had organised plenty of promotional events in the past, but tonight was an exclusive evening for some of the wealthiest and most influential people in the country, and Asha had a lot riding on its success.

While the others she originally arrived with had focused on the vineyard, Asha had spent months putting tonight together under Isabelle's direction. It was an important occasion for Standing Stone, one that guaranteed plenty of orders for the year ahead, but the initial weeks had been difficult. Apparently, the young woman who organised last year's signature event had left Standing Stone under a cloud, so Asha had no handover and nothing to build on. But she was determined to outdo her predecessor tonight and make Isabelle proud.

The manor house had been transformed under her direction, and as Asha walked up the path, she couldn't help but feel a surge of pride.

The grand entryway was a riot of autumnal splendour,

with garlands of grape vines winding around the banisters and columns, their leaves a patchwork of green and gold. Clusters of ripe fruit hung just out of reach, their skins gleaming in the soft light of hundreds of candles. The spicy aroma of mulled cider overlaid the warm scent of wine and earth. It was as if the essence of the vineyard had been distilled and poured into the house, blurring the lines between inside and out.

Isabelle walked down the grand staircase, resplendent in a shimmering gown of midnight blue and silver. "Ready?" she asked, her eyes glinting with anticipation.

Asha nodded, taking a deep breath. "As I'll ever be."

The first guests soon arrived in a parade of sleek cars purring up the gravel driveway. As the waitstaff served wine and canapés made from local produce, Asha recognised faces from the carefully curated guest list. A powerful politician, as well as a tech billionaire, and a celebrated actress, all greeted Isabelle with warmth, clearly having attended previous events.

The manor house was soon alive with the low hum of conversation and the gentle clink of wine glasses, as a jazz band played in the main entrance hall.

Isabelle managed to speak to everyone at least briefly, as Nate moved amongst the guests, pouring out one of the more premium wines. He only offered it to some people, pointedly ignoring others — yet another social hierarchy within this already exclusive gathering.

As the event continued, she constantly circulated, making sure everything ran smoothly.

In the grand dining room, long tables groaned under the weight of the feast. Whole roasted pigs, their skins crackling and golden. Platters overflowing with local cheeses, crusty artisanal bread, and vegetables of every kind. It was a display of pastoral abundance, a celebration of the harvest in all its glory. Although it was no doubt rustic for those more used to the minimalism currently fashionable in London, this was so much more authentic. People wanted genuine experiences these days, especially the rich, and Asha intended to give them something to talk about — and, of course, make sure they knew she was the one behind it.

She walked through into the main drawing room, which had been transformed into a living vineyard. Real grape vines climbed the walls, their tendrils reaching across the ceiling to create a canopy of leaves and fruit, like an ancient temple dedicated to Bacchus, the Roman god of wine and fertility.

Guests reclined on low couches draped with rich fabric, and the air was hazy with smoke from clay pipes, the tobacco blend infused with herbs from the vineyard. Nate had prepared the blend especially for the event, but he insisted on keeping the recipe secret.

The band played on. There was dancing and more food, and fire breathers, and much wine drunk from the cellars. Asha made sure that she and other strategically placed staff took plenty of photos that would be perfect for the website and social media. It would look like the event of the season and she would make sure that those who weren't here had some serious FOMO.

Around eleven, the cars pulled up and most of the guests were ushered off into the night. They were waved away by enthusiastic staff, who were soon gone as well until only Asha remained along with Isabelle, Nate, and a small hand-selected group of revellers.

The main party was over, but the truly exclusive event was about to begin. Isabelle had forbidden any photos or recording of this more intimate gathering, which only served to make Asha more curious about what it might entail, since Isabelle had kept the plans for this after-party to herself.

As the clock struck midnight, Isabelle led the small group into the drawing room. The guests were merry with wine and food, but the atmosphere became serious as Isabelle raised her hands for silence.

"Tonight, we stand in a place where the veil between worlds grows thin, where the ancient power of the vine holds sway."

A hush fell over the crowd, every eye fixed on Isabelle as she reached up and plucked a single grape.

"For millennia, wine has been more than mere drink. It is a sacrament through which we commune with our darkness and the sacred energy that runs through this land. Tonight, you will taste the culmination of that tradition. The Horned God's Share."

Nate walked forward, holding a single wine bottle with reverence. The glass was so dark it seemed to absorb the surrounding light and on its label, a simple line drawing of a horned skull emerged from lush vines.

While the wine that Nate shared amongst some guests earlier had been exclusive, this vintage was so rare that it was only available to invited guests for tasting twice a year. The bottles were sold under blind auction and rumoured to reach extravagant sums.

Nate gently placed the bottle on a small table beside Isabelle as she continued. "The Horned God's Share is more than just wine. It is liquid history, the essence of this land and those who live and work on it distilled into drops of the divine."

She raised an eyebrow and gave an almost lecherous smile. "You will taste heaven, my friends, and then you have the rest of the night to take yourself there."

As Isabelle wove a spell of words over the audience, Asha looked around at the guests who remained, recognising many of them.

The chief constable, the highest-ranking police officer in the county, his cheeks flushed with wine and anticipation. A bishop stood nearby, although he had removed the golden cross around his neck that Asha had noticed earlier in the evening. The tech billionaire sat next to an old money aristocrat, all united in their desire for the exclusive, the forbidden.

It was mostly men left now, and Asha noticed that a few of them looked at her with interest. These were people accustomed to power, to getting exactly what they wanted. She would have to make sure they didn't get too handsy later.

Nate brought in a wide, shallow tray with small hand-made cups resting upon it, their surfaces rough and uneven. The candlelight caught the edges of the vessels, highlighting cracks and imperfections that spoke of centuries past.

"Roman?" Asha heard someone whisper.

"Etruscan, more likely," another guest murmured in response.

The ancient cups seemed to absorb the flickering light, creating pools of shadow in their bowls. Asha wondered how many now dead and buried worshippers had sipped from these very vessels over the generations.

"From earth we come, and to earth we return." Isabelle lifted the dark bottle of the Horned God's Share. "But tonight, we transcend our earthly bonds."

With reverent care, she poured a small measure of wine into each cup.

It was thicker than normal wine, and the dark liquid seemed to move with a life of its own, pooling in the bottom of each cup, its surface as still and black as obsidian.

As Isabelle poured, she chanted words in an ancient language, both guttural and lyrical, that made the hairs on the back of Asha's neck stand on end.

"Horned One, Master of the Wild Hunt. We offer you this night's bounty." Isabelle raised her cup.

The candles flickered violently, flames dancing as if stirred by an unfelt wind. Their shadows leaped and twisted on the walls, taking on strange shapes that stalked through the room as if searching for prey.

"We ask for your blessing," Isabelle continued, her eyes gleaming in the unsteady light. "Open us with your savage heart and let us be untamed in your presence."

As Nate passed around the cups and each guest took one, some with shaky hands. A hush fell over the room and the air grew heavy and expectant, pressing down on Asha's chest until each breath felt like a struggle.

It must be the scent of the wine making her heady. It was rich and earthy, with undertones of ripe fruit and something more primal that lingered at the back of her throat.

As Isabelle raised her cup to inhale its bouquet, the guests followed suit, their eyes fluttering closed as expressions of pure bliss washed over their faces. Sighs of pleasure and anticipation rippled through the gathering.

"Breathe in the essence of the vine," Isabelle instructed, holding her cup before her like a chalice. "Let it fill your senses and take you deeper."

The guests seemed to fall into a trance-like state, swaying gently, as if moved by an unseen current. The tech billionaire's fingers trembled as he clutched his cup, while the bishop's face took on an almost beatific glow.

Isabelle raised her vessel high, the surface of the dark liquid catching the candlelight for a brief moment. "Drink now to the Horned God. May his wild blood flow through our veins and bless us for the Wild Hunt."

As one, the assembled guests lifted their cups.

Asha held her breath, watching as they tipped their heads back and drank deeply. The room fell silent save for the sound of sipping and the occasional gasp of pleasure.

The chief constable was the first to lower his cup, his eyes wide and unfocused. A thin trickle of wine ran from the corner of his mouth, staining his collar crimson. He made no move to wipe it away. Instead, he ran his tongue slowly over his lips as if to savour every drop.

The aristocrat let out a low moan, and his cup slipped

from suddenly slack fingers onto the carpeted floor as he shuddered in ecstasy.

What the hell was in this wine?

Asha felt a touch on her back and turned to find Nate with a clay cup in his hand, a few centimetres of wine within.

He offered it to her. "Try some. You deserve it after all your hard work."

The wine looked almost alive as he turned the cup and it caught the light. For a moment, Asha thought she saw faces in its depths — ancient, wild visages that vanished as quickly as they appeared.

"I couldn't possibly," Asha demurred, even as her fingers itched to reach for the cup. "I'm still working."

Nate smiled, and in his eyes was a dark promise. He leaned closer. "The work is done." He pressed the cup into her hand. "Now is the time to reap the reward."

Asha took the cup and raised it, inhaling deeply as the others had done. The aroma was intoxicating — ripe berries and sun-warmed earth, with hints of smoke and something mineral.

Above her, the vines seemed to move closer, their tendrils reaching out as if to caress the assembled guests. If this vision came from just the scent of the wine, what would the taste do to her?

"Drink," Nate whispered. "Let the Horned God come. Taste the spirit of Standing Stone. How can you understand the vineyard unless you experience it?"

Asha's hand trembled as she raised the cup, closed her eyes, and took her first taste.

CHAPTER 25

IN THE FIRST SIP, Asha tasted berry notes layered with wild herbs and something darker, a metallic tang that intensified before dropping into a sense of crushed leaves under ancient vines.

The wine was full-bodied, and as she drank the cup down, Asha relaxed into wonder at its complexity. It was as if birth and fermentation and decay all happened simultaneously, and each mouthful contained the abundance of life in the vineyard. Asha had heard the term *terroir*, but until now, she had never really understood how a place could be so embodied in a wine.

The Horned God's Share burned a fiery path down her throat, and the room around her pulsed and shifted as her perception deepened. Colours became more vivid, and sounds sharpened and clarified, as if her animal senses were coming to life.

Asha blinked, refocusing on the room and those around her. The flush on their cheeks, the wild light in their eyes. The power of the vine clearly touched all who drank.

She felt the warmth of Nate's hand on the small of her back, his touch electric even through the fabric of her dress. He lightly ran his fingers over the curve of her buttocks and Asha gasped at the intensity of the sensation.

"This is the gift of Standing Stone," he murmured, his breath hot against her ear. He moved behind her and pulled her back against him, his hands exploring her body with feather light touches. Others could see them, but Asha didn't even care. She was lost in sensation, and around them, all were lost in their own pleasure.

A laugh bubbled up from the crowd, high and wild, as the tech billionaire threw his head back in abandon. His pupils were wide, leaving only a thin ring of colour around inky black pools. He began to sway, his movements becoming more fluid and animalistic with each passing moment.

The bishop was on his knees, hands raised in supplication, as he muttered what sounded like a prayer. But the words that spilled from his lips were no holy litany. They were guttural and primal, an invocation to forces far older than any church.

The celebration transformed into something wilder, more primal, with couples and groups taking pleasure in each other as Isabelle glided through the chaos like a dark goddess, her gown now seeming to be woven from the shadows that danced at the edges of the room. Wherever she passed, the frenzy intensified.

The chief constable climbed on top of a table, wearing a crown of twisted vines and small bones as he thrust into one reveller. At their feet, others writhed in ecstasy, fingers clawing at the earth as if trying to sink roots into the vineyard floor beneath.

Asha's heart raced, pounding a frantic rhythm against her ribs as Nate held her close against him. He had one arm around her waist, almost forcing her to watch what was happening, while his other hand teased her to heights of pleasure.

While his touch hypnotised part of her, Asha also sensed an edge of danger in the room.

It was slipping out of control.

A primal instinct deep inside screamed at her to run, but her limbs were leaden. She couldn't move.

She caught sight of her reflection in the mirror across the room. Her eyes were wild, her hair a tangle of leaves and vine tendrils. A flush had spread across her cheeks and down her neck, disappearing beneath her dress. She looked feral, dangerous.

Beautiful.

Behind her, Nate's eyes met hers in the mirror and in them, she saw a hunger that she, too, felt rising inside.

The music, which had faded to background noise, suddenly swelled into the haunting sounds of pipes and drums, a primal rhythm that spoke of hunt and harvest, of life and death entwined. The melody was discordant, yet it resonated through Asha's bones, calling to something ancient and wild within her.

In the midst of the revelry, Isabelle led a small roe deer into the room, and tethered it to the table. It trembled, clearly terrified, huddling as close as possible to the wood, and Asha felt a chill at what it must surely represent.

Isabelle began to chant ancient words with guttural sounds. The other guests took up her chant, their voices blending into a chorus that made the air vibrate.

A gust of wind swept through the room, extinguishing half the candles, and the scent of crushed grapes and damp soil grew stronger, mingling with the musk of sweat and desire.

Shadows cast by the guests stretched and twisted into forms that were more animal than human. Antlers and horns sprouted from some, while others had tails that lashed the air.

In the darkness beyond the manor house, Asha heard the sound of hooves, distant but drawing nearer. The baying of feral hounds echoed in her mind, accompanied by the rustle of leaves and the snapping of branches.

"The Wild Hunt grows near," Isabelle called out. "The Horned One comes."

The thunderous sound of hooves grew louder, reverberating through the manor house with such force that the walls trembled. The baying of hounds became a cacophony, their otherworldly howls echoing with an edge of mania.

The walls of the manor house dissolved and melted away, and the revellers now stood in an ancient vineyard bathed in moonlight. The vines twisted and writhed around them, sending out tendrils to wrap around their limbs and caress bare flesh.

As Asha's eyes adjusted to the dark, a shadowy figure emerged from the trees.

He was huge and muscled, a primal creature with horns and a crown of twisted vines. All kinds of beasts surrounded him — many-antlered deer, dark fey steeds, and hounds with huge limbs, slavering jaws wide with hunger. Although she couldn't see his eyes, Asha sensed his power.

His gaze fell upon her, and she gasped at the brief vision she saw there.

Blood. So much blood.

Isabelle turned to look at Asha, her eyes narrowing as she noted Nate's embrace, but then she smiled. "The Horned God sees you. A blessing indeed."

She looked pointedly at Nate, and Asha felt his arms tighten around her. Was he protecting — or restraining — her?

Isabelle raised her arms and called out, "Oh, Horned One, accept our sacrifice."

The chief constable let out a howl that was answered by the baying hounds, as the bishop whirled in abandon, calling out in the guttural words of the land.

Isabelle picked up a ritual blade, its bone handle decorated with horned creatures. She approached the deer from behind and yanked its head back.

With a swift, practiced motion, she drew the blade across its throat. Blood sprayed forth, dark and rich in the moonlight. The metallic scent filled the air, mingling with the earthy aroma of the vineyard.

Isabelle laid the animal down and sliced it further, opening its chest and innards and cutting through the sinews of its limbs.

The revellers howled and fell upon the carcass like a pack of wild animals. Hands that only hours ago had delicately held wine glasses now tore at flesh and sinew. The chief constable, his face now smeared with blood, ripped a chunk of meat free with his teeth. The bishop, all traces of piety gone, fought with the billionaire over a choice morsel.

Asha watched — horrified yet unable to look away — as the carcass was savagely torn apart by the animals they had become.

Throughout it all, Isabelle moved through the group, her knife flashing as she directed the dismemberment. She was a pagan priestess overseeing a sacred rite, her movements graceful even as the frenzy raged about her.

The stink of blood and raw flesh was underlaid with the aroma of wine and fermenting grapes on the edge of rot. Asha's head swam, her senses overwhelmed by the barbaric spectacle.

Enough.

She had to get out of there.

She tried to break free from Nate's embrace, but he held her more tightly, his iron grip immovable.

Asha screamed, but no words came out, just a kind of moan. As she writhed in his grip, she felt tendrils of the vines circling her ankles, constricting as they wound up her legs.

Isabelle turned from the carcass, her lips and chin stained crimson as she met Asha's gaze. She gave a feral smile as she gulped down out a bloody chunk of meat, licking her lips with pleasure.

"The Horned God requires more," Isabelle called out. "It is time for the true sacrifice."

The revellers looked up, their hands and faces covered with gore, eyes wide, teeth bared.

As one, they turned to stare at Asha.

She twisted and writhed, heart pounding as she tried desperately to escape. But she was bound in place by the savage vines and Nate's bestial strength, and almost paralysed by whatever strange drug was in the wine.

Isabelle picked up the ritual knife and recited the guttural prayers once more.

She stalked closer as the vines curled higher around Asha's body, their sinewy power pulling her down to her knees.

Nate let her go and stepped away, allowing Isabelle to stand behind her.

Asha wept as she tried to escape the bonds of the vines, but they constricted tighter and tighter, tethering her to the land beneath.

She felt Isabelle's almost gentle hand on her forehead, pulling her neck back as the chant rose to a crescendo.

A flash of the silver blade.

A warm rush of blood.

The Horned God took his sacrifice.

CHAPTER 26

THE MORNING SUN SLANTED through the windows of the manor house, its cheerful radiance at odds with the chaos within as Rebecca picked her way carefully through the debris-strewn hallway. The click of her boots on the hardwood floor seemed unnaturally loud in the post-celebration hush.

It had clearly been an excellent party.

The grand entrance hall, which had been a verdant wonderland last night, now looked like a battlefield where nature and debauchery had waged a violent war. Wilted vines, their leaves crushed and torn, hung limply from the curling banisters, and sticky puddles of spilled wine stained the antique rugs.

The sour note of stale alcohol mingled with the cloying sweetness of overripe fruit and the bitterness of tobacco smoke. Underlying it all, the aroma of sex and sweat — and the metallic stench of blood. What the hell happened here last night?

Rebecca made her way up to the library, intent on working on her architectural plans before her next shift in the vineyard. She wove past broken glass and leftover food plates, and tried to ignore the revellers who hadn't made it home.

A man in a rumpled tuxedo lay sprawled across a chaise lounge. His bow tie was undone and his shirt lay ripped open, allowing a glimpse of bloody scratches across his chest. In a shadowed corner, a woman in a designer gown slept curled up like a cat, her hair a wild tangle framing her face, her lips and hands stained crimson.

Isabelle's bedroom was on the same floor as the library, and as Rebecca passed, the door opened.

Isabelle emerged, wrapped loosely in a black silk robe, her silver hair tousled from sleep. Before she pulled the door closed behind her, Rebecca glimpsed a masculine form in the bed — Nate, his muscular back unmistakable even in the dim light.

Isabelle smiled at Rebecca as she stretched languidly. "Morning. You're in early."

"I'm keen to finish the last stage of the plans. Sorry to disturb you."

Isabelle waved a hand, dismissing her concern. "No, it's fine. Carry on. I'm sorry about the state of the place." She arched one eyebrow. "It was quite the party, even by my standards."

As Isabelle headed downstairs for coffee, Rebecca walked on down the corridor. Then she turned back and called down the stairs.

"Have you seen Asha? She didn't come back last night."

Isabelle looked up from the grand staircase as a gust of wind billowed the loose black robe about her form.

For a moment, Rebecca thought she saw the tattered wings and dark feathers of the Beltane Night Gathering as Isabelle's face transformed into something more feral and ancient. Was that a streak of blood on her neck? And dirt under her fingernails?

Rebecca took a deep breath and shook her head to clear the image. This place was taking its toll, for sure.

Isabelle pulled her gown more tightly around her body.

"The evening was an incredible success for Asha. One of our special guests — the owner of a prestigious vineyard in France — was so impressed, he offered her a position. Much higher pay than I can afford, and an immediate start, to help with seasonal events. She left with him after the party."

Rebecca frowned, an uneasy feeling settling in her stomach. "She left? Without saying goodbye?"

Isabelle shrugged. "It all happened rather quickly. You know how these things can be in the heat of the moment. I'm sure she'll be in touch once she's settled."

Rebecca forced a smile. "Yes, of course. I'm so glad the night was a success."

As she turned away, her stomach churned with an edge of doubt.

First Liam, then Helen, and now Asha. All gone without a word, vanishing in the night as if they had never been there at all.

Ben's words from that midsummer morning on the hill came back to her. "Surely you've noticed that not everything is normal here?"

With his remembered words on her lips, Rebecca hurried to the library, which was mercifully untouched by the excesses of last night. Even so, something of the tainted atmosphere pervaded the space, and she felt uneasy.

Her plans still lay on the table, their organic curves and botanical lines representing hope for the future of the vineyard. But around her, the shelves were filled with knowledge from its past, with books packed in dense rows all the way to the ceiling. Their cracked spines and leather smell now seemed to have an undercurrent of decay, as if the knowledge contained within had ripened past its prime and now descended into rot and putrefaction.

Rebecca looked around, seeing the library with a new perspective. Titles that had once seemed quaint or even scholarly now took on a more sinister aspect.

The Golden Bough by Sir James George Frazer was an encyclopaedia of rural customs and superstition, but it also had chapters on human sacrifice and ritual murder, practiced by cultures across the world and throughout history.

In the fiction section, Rebecca spotted an original 1978 paperback of *The Wicker Man* by Robin Hardy and Anthony Shaffer. The story of a pagan community luring an outsider to his fiery death suddenly felt less like fantasy and more like a warning.

In the shelves dedicated to wine and viticulture, one book's leather binding seemed darker than the others, more worn perhaps. Rebecca pulled it out. *Liber Ivonis*. The name meant nothing to Rebecca, but the book radiated a malevolent aura of blasphemy and dark secrets.

As she walked around the room, other objects took on new significance.

An antique globe in the corner, whose painted surface depicted a world both familiar and strange, as gods and monsters roamed its lands and seas. An ornate letter opener shaped like a curved dagger on the desk, with flakes of what could be red wax — or dried blood — on its blade.

And watching over everything, in a glass cabinet full of figurines, Rebecca spotted a creature of tarnished metal, half-man and half-beast, its hoof pressing the head of a sacrifice into the earth, while it raised its horned antlers to the sky.

In that moment she realised that everything was not normal here, but she had kept denying the truth of it. So much was wonderful and special about the vineyard, and Rebecca felt as if Standing Stone could truly become her home. A place where she could be a useful member of the community, enjoy the abundance of natural life, and use her architectural skills to create a beautiful legacy.

She desperately wanted Ben to be wrong, but as good a liar as Isabelle must be, Asha's disappearance was one step too far. The young woman was a similar age to Grace when she disappeared, and now Rebecca felt a deep foreboding that her sister's fate was just as entwined with this place.

An icy breath of wind blew in through the half-open window, lifting the papers from the desk.

As Rebecca grabbed at them and weighed them back down, she wondered if she could even work in here again. The atmosphere felt so malevolent now.

She took a deep breath. Come on, these are only books, whatever dark words they might contain.

The thought took hold as Rebecca considered what else the books might contain within them.

This library was the heart of the Manor House, but rarely used. If there was a list of women bound to the vineyard as she had found in the grimoire, perhaps there was a list of victims or sacrifices, if indeed there had been any over the years.

Rebecca crept back to the door and opened it a crack, listening to the sounds of the house. She did not want to be disturbed.

Moans of pleasure came from Isabelle's room and it sounded like she and Nate might be busy for some time.

With a shaky breath, Rebecca pushed the door closed again, then wheeled the ladder over to the top shelf where the grimoire lay.

She climbed the rungs, stretching high up, and pulled down the books on either side of the grimoire. There were tomes on arcane practices in viticulture and aspects of rural customs that some would claim were witchcraft, but nothing that seemed applicable.

Rebecca moved down to the next shelf, where a series of Greek tragedies stood packed closely together in matching maroon leather bindings.

They were mostly in pristine condition, as if no one had ever touched them, but one had a spine that was cracked and faded from regular use.

Rebecca pulled it out. The cover was adorned with intricate vines that writhed and twisted together, their tendrils stained a deep rust colour, and the gilt lettering on the cover gleamed in the morning sun.

The Bacchae by Euripides.

A memory stirred in the recesses of her mind, fragments of a long-ago Classics lecture bubbling to the surface.

The play centred around Dionysus, the god of wine and ecstatic revelry. Known to the Romans as Bacchus, the deity embodied the wild, untamed aspects of nature and the extremes of human passion.

In the play, Dionysus arrived in Thebes to establish his cult, and drove the women of the city into a mania of ecstatic worship, while those who resisted his divine power were severely punished. At the story's climax, a group of maenads — the god's frenzied female followers — savagely rip apart what they think is a stag, but is really Pentheus, King of Thebes.

Had the ancient playwright glimpsed some eternal truth about the dark undercurrents that ran beneath the surface of civilisation?

Or were the guardians of Standing Stone drawing inspiration from these age-old tales of divine madness and sacrificial violence?

Perhaps there was some indication inside.

With trembling hands, Rebecca opened the book.

Her breath caught in her throat.

The pages had been hollowed out to create a secret compartment within. Nestled in the hidden cavity lay an ancient key, its metal dark with age, its handle covered in intricate engravings. Twisting vines, runes she recognised from the grimoire, and, of course, the Horned God.

The markings matched the door to the mysterious room down in the wine cellar.

Rebecca picked up the key and weighed it in her hand.

Whatever was behind that door must surely reveal more about what was going on here, and perhaps a clue to the disappearances of her fellow workers, and even to Grace.

The sounds from along the corridor were loud and rhythmic now. It wouldn't be long before Isabelle emerged.

Rebecca didn't have time now, but she was determined to use the key to find out once and for all whether Standing Stone had a heart of sacrificial darkness or whether it was all just rural traditions she didn't understand as an outsider.

Rebecca placed the key back inside the book and slotted *The Bacchae* into its place before hurrying down the ladder and moving it to the other side of the library to hide her search.

A few moments later, the creak of a door and the sound of approaching footsteps came from along the corridor.

Rebecca stood behind the desk and bent over a page of plans, her heart hammering.

The library door swung open and Isabelle walked in, the black robe cinched tightly at her waist.

"Still here?" Isabelle's tone was casual, but her gaze was sharp. "I thought you'd be out in the vineyard by now. I'm heading for the shower and the cleaners are on their way, so perhaps it's best if you head out, too."

Rebecca forced a smile as she gathered her notes. "Of course, I'll just finish up."

Isabelle nodded as she scanned the room as if searching for anything out of place. "Well, don't let me keep you. And Rebecca, remember that curiosity can be dangerous out here in the country. Some books — and some doors — are best left unopened."

The threat in her words was unmistakable.

Rebecca nodded, her mouth dry. "Of course," she managed to say. "I'll keep that in mind."

Isabelle waited for Rebecca to leave the library and then closed the door after her.

As Rebecca walked down the stairs and out into the day, she felt Isabelle's gaze on her back, but despite the woman's warning, Rebecca was determined to use that key.

She would know the truth. She just had to find the right time.

CHAPTER 27

THE VINEYARD HUMMED WITH the frenetic energy of harvest season, and the once-neat rows of vines now bustled with activity. Local community members and itinerant workers moved swiftly between them, carefully selecting and snipping off the ripe clusters of grapes. The heady aroma of fruit on the cusp of fermentation mingled with the earthy scent of freshly turned soil and the tang of sweat.

Rebecca found herself swept up in the whirlwind of activity. Her days began before dawn, joining the other workers in the misty fields. She'd grown adept at handling the razor-sharp secateurs, her fingers nimble as she sought the perfect bunches. The satisfying snip of stem giving way to blade had become a comforting rhythm, punctuated by the occasional call of "Basket!" as workers filled their containers to the brim with plump, juicy grapes and shouted for new vessels that would then be carted back to the fermentation sheds.

The work was hard and left Rebecca with aching muscles. She fell into her bunk each night exhausted, wondering if she could make it through another day of strenuous work. But there was also a sense of camaraderie among the harvesters that made the long hours bearable, and even fun at times. They shared water and jokes, comparing the size of their grape clusters and competing to fill their baskets the fastest.

As the days wore on, Rebecca found herself yearning for the quiet sanctuary of the library, though now the thought of it was tinged with a hollow ache. She missed the musty smell of old books, the way the sunlight once slanted through the tall windows, illuminating motes of dust that danced in the air. But now, those moments felt distant, unreachable, as if the library had become a ghost of itself—tainted by shadows she could no longer ignore. The solace she once found there had been fractured, but she still needed to get back in and revisit the book and the key. There just hadn't been the opportunity.

"Rebecca," Isabelle called out one morning across the yard. "I've had your plans and drawings moved to the administration block. I need your help with harvest data entry, which is a better use of your skills. It'll be easier for you to work on the computer there now that you're done with your research."

The implication was clear and Rebecca nodded, forcing a smile even as her heart sank. "Of course, that makes sense. Thank you."

On the rare morning she worked on the plans, Rebecca now felt unsettled. She couldn't shake the feeling that she was being watched.

Every time she glanced out the window, she half-expected to see Isabelle's silvery head poking around the corner, checking up on her. Was her access to the library being deliberately restricted? Did Isabelle know what she had found? Perhaps the key had even been moved. Rebecca was desperate to get back inside and find out.

While she waited for an opportunity, she focused on inputting data into the harvest tracking records, which tracked the batches of grapes through the winemaking process. It was strange to have such technological capabilities alongside the older ways of the vineyard, and it underscored how much Standing Stone Cellars aimed for a perfect blend of old and new in their wines.

The vineyard was bustling with activity. In the winery, workers were busy with the delicate process of whole-cluster pressing for the sparkling wines. The grapes had been harvested slightly earlier, with higher acidity and lower sugar levels, perfect for creating the crisp, effervescent wines that Standing Stone had won awards for.

In other sections, the focus was on red varietals, where the grapes were left on the vine longer, allowing them to develop deeper, more complex flavours.

The late-harvest wines of Bacchus and Solaris were a specialty of Standing Stone, left on the vine long past the main harvest, sometimes even into the first frost. The result was intensely sweet, concentrated fruit that would become dessert wines. It was a risky process, as the grapes were vulnerable to rot or animal predation, so they required constant vigilance and a deep understanding of the vineyard's microclimate. Those late harvest grapes were the last left on the vines, and Nate and Isabelle fussed over the fields, testing the Brix levels sometimes multiple times a day.

One afternoon, a commotion outside drew Rebecca's attention from her data entry work.

She glanced out the window to see Nate and Isabelle in the yard, talking to one of the workers who managed the late harvest. Their expressions were grave, and Rebecca could see their tension even from a distance. A group of workers gathered around, also looking worried. Clearly, something serious had happened.

Isabelle's expression was set in grim determination as she pointed towards the fields and shouted orders. Workers scattered, rushing to gather equipment as Nate jogged towards the equipment shed, emerging moments later with a backpack sprayer slung over his shoulder.

As the group walked quickly in the direction of the farthest vine rows, Rebecca's heart raced.

This was her chance. Perhaps her only opportunity.

She wouldn't have much time, but it would have to be long enough.

Rebecca slipped out of the office and took a roundabout path to the manor house, skirting the edges of the buildings to avoid being seen. As she approached the grand old structure, she couldn't shake the feeling that the carved faces in the stonework watched her, their eyes following her every move.

The back door creaked as she eased it open, the sound unnaturally loud in the quiet house. Rebecca froze, listening for any sign she'd been heard. But the manor house remained still and silent.

She hurried through the corridors, her footsteps muffled by the thick carpets, and headed up to the library. The room was cool and dim, with heavy curtains drawn to keep out the autumn chill.

She rolled the ladder over to the shelf and climbed up. *The Bacchae* was still there — but would it be empty?

With her heart pounding, she pulled out the hollowed book and opened it.

The key lay hidden in its compartment.

With a sigh of relief, Rebecca picked it up. It seemed heavier this time, the metal cool against her palm, the intricate etchings on its surface catching the dim light.

She slipped the key in her pocket and slid the book back into place before hurrying down the main stairs and down the narrower flight into the wine cellar.

The scent of earth and aged wine grew stronger as she descended the worn stone staircase. The temperature dropped with each step, and Rebecca shivered, wishing she'd thought to bring her jacket.

At the bottom, the lighting was low to protect the wines, and she paused a moment to let her eyes adjust to the gloom.

Rows upon rows of wine racks stretched out before her, with bottles aligned like dark sentinels in the shadows.

Rebecca hurried between the racks, her fingers brushing against the cool glass as she made her way deeper into the cellar.

The door was at the far end, hidden behind the oldest vintages, and although she had been down here to fetch wine since that first tour with Isabelle, Rebecca had not stood in front of the ancient wood since then.

Now she examined it with a fresh perspective.

The ornate vine carvings seemed to curl and writhe around the horned figure in the low light, and Rebecca's hand shook slightly as she pulled out the key and inserted it into the lock.

She tried to twist it. Nothing happened. It didn't even turn.

For a terrifying moment, she thought this had all been for nothing.

But then she jiggled it a little and felt the mechanism engage.

The lock clicked open.

CHAPTER 28

Rᴇʙᴇᴄᴄᴀ ᴘᴜsʜᴇᴅ ᴛʜᴇ ᴅᴏᴏʀ open as the ancient hinges groaned in protest. The sound echoed through the cavernous space beyond, sending a shiver down her spine. As she stepped across the threshold, the temperature plummeted, and her breath formed ghostly wisps in the frigid air.

The low lighting from the wine cellar cast her shadow into the space beyond, in a distorted silhouette. Rebecca's heart pounded in her chest as she peered into the gloom, trying to make sense of what lay before her.

At first glance, the stone chamber appeared similar to the rest of the wine cellar, its walls hewn from the same ancient rock. But instead of racks laden with bottles, there were rows upon rows of glass display cabinets. They stretched into the darkness, their contents obscured by shadow, many of them covered with a fine layer of dust.

Rebecca frowned. She had expected some kind of pagan altar and maybe a floor stained with the blood of ritual sacrifice, but this looked more like a museum, assorted curiosities collected by the vineyard's owners over generations.

She fumbled for a light switch and found a lever. She pulled it down.

A buzz, a crackle, and the chamber came alive with a soft hum.

Small lamps mounted on the sides of each cabinet flickered to life with a warm glow that hinted at the treasures within rather than fully revealing them.

As her eyes adjusted, Rebecca made out more details. Each cabinet was meticulously labelled with a range of years, the dates etched into small brass plaques on the front.

She walked closer, her footsteps echoing in the silence, and noticed that the years stretched back in time as the cabinets receded into the depths of the chamber.

The glass cabinet doors reflected distorted visions of her face as she passed by. In one, her eyes were large, dark pools that seemed to swallow the light. In another, her mouth stretched into an unnatural grin, teeth gleaming. Rebecca shuddered and averted her gaze from the dark carnival likeness.

Once she had determined that there was nothing in the chamber other than the cabinets, Rebecca leaned in to examine the contents of the nearest one.

Each shelf represented a year and had a series of what appeared to be mundane objects lying on top. A tarnished button, a scrap of faded fabric, a lock of hair tied with a fraying ribbon. Every item was labelled with painstaking care, bearing a name and a date in spidery handwriting alongside the runes of the Horned God.

As she moved from cabinet to cabinet, Rebecca's confusion grew.

The objects seemed random and intensely personal. A child's marble with swirling colours dulled by time; a woman's earring made of a single pearl dangling from a bent wire. Other shelves had fragments of bone and yellowed teeth, and one contained scraps of what looked like parchment covered in indecipherable script.

The deeper Rebecca ventured into the chamber, the older the artefacts became.

A cabinet from the early 1900s contained Victorian-era

trinkets — a mourning brooch with a twist of dark hair, a tiny pair of leather baby shoes, a pressed flower that looked as if it would crumble to dust with the slightest touch.

Further back still, she found objects that spoke of a more distant past. A Roman coin, green with age. A shard of pottery daubed with ochre dye. A stone arrowhead, wickedly sharp despite the millennia that had passed since its creation.

As she examined each cabinet, a growing sense of unease settled in the pit of Rebecca's stomach. These were not museum curiosities. They were personal mementoes — or trophies.

The realisation made her gasp and Rebecca hurried back through the chamber, her breath catching in her throat as she found the cabinet for the current year. She bent closer to look inside.

Liam's olive wood cross necklace.

A page of Helen's botanical notebook.

The ornate Montblanc pen that Asha's dad had given to her.

Rebecca stifled a gasp, her hand over her mouth at the implication of what had befallen her fellow workers. The words in the grimoire surfaced in her mind. Rituals of binding and sacrifice to ensure a bountiful harvest.

She spun around slowly, taking in the enormity of the chamber. How many lives were represented here? How many sacrifices made to the land in exchange for abundance?

She had to know whether Grace was part of this terrible legacy.

Rebecca walked slowly back down the cabinet row, counting back the years to when her sister disappeared. With nausea rising in her throat, she opened the cabinet to see what lay within.

A plastic hair clip with a butterfly design.

A small metal box emblazoned with a Bible verse.

And there, in the middle, a wooden triple moon pendant hanging from a leather cord.

Tears spilled down Rebecca's cheeks as she reached out for the pendant. She had seen it around Grace's neck countless times as her sister fidgeted with it when deep in thought, a smile on her lips.

It was definitely hers.

Grace had died at Standing Stone.

With shaking hands, Rebecca lifted the pendant out and sank to the floor with it clutched between her palms. She sobbed as she closed her eyes and thought of her sister. Had she suffered? What had they done with her body?

But even as she considered the possibilities, Rebecca knew in her heart where the bones must be.

In the forbidden part of the vineyard. The only place she had not visited.

Rebecca wept then for herself. For her blindness and her willingness to ignore the signs, to believe in the vineyard's beauty without questioning the darkness that lay beneath.

She was so lost in her sorrow that she didn't hear the approaching footsteps until it was too late.

The heavy door to the vault swung open.

Rebecca looked up, blinking through her tears. Isabelle stood framed in the doorway.

For a moment, the two women stared at each other in silence.

Then Isabelle's face crumpled, a look of profound sorrow washing over her features. "Oh, my poor girl," she whispered, crossing the room in swift strides.

Before Rebecca could react, Isabelle knelt and wrapped her in a warm embrace.

The older woman's arms were strong and comforting, her scent a mixture of earth and flowers that Rebecca associated with the vineyard itself.

For a heartbeat, Rebecca remained stiff in Isabelle's arms, her mind reeling with conflicting emotion.

This woman was responsible for Grace's murder and for countless other deaths, and yet the comfort she offered was so needed.

With a choked sob, Rebecca gave in.

She leaned into Isabelle's embrace, her tears flowing freely once more. Isabelle held her close, one hand stroking Rebecca's hair in a gesture so maternal it made Rebecca's heart ache.

"Let it out, my dear," Isabelle murmured. "I know the pain you feel. Let me take some of it from you."

As Rebecca's sobs finally receded, Isabelle pulled away from their embrace. She looked much older down here, the years lying more heavily upon her.

"I'm sorry you had to find out like this, and I know you must have many questions. You deserve answers, especially as I hoped to bring you down when you were ready. What we do here is not an easy thing, and we have all lost loved ones. We have all made sacrifices."

Isabelle looked down the row of cabinets at one from several decades ago, as the fingertips of her right hand touched her bare ring finger on the left. She sighed. "Our practices are hard to accept, but they are necessary. I hope you will come to see that."

Rebecca took a shuddering breath and gestured to the rows of cabinets. "How can this possibly be necessary?"

Isabelle settled herself next to Rebecca on the stone floor. "Standing Stone is not just a section of agricultural land like any other. There is something old and hungry beneath the earth that has been here since before humans walked this land. The Horned God is its latest incarnation, but it has been worshipped under many guises for millennia. With appropriate sacrifice, the soil is imbued with extraordinary depth, providing the grapes with the richness of an unmatched terroir."

Isabelle paused and gazed into the distance. "The guardians tried other methods, of course. Elaborate rituals with symbolic offerings. Animal sacrifices. But in those years, the crops failed, the vines withered, and the land became poisoned. Children became sick, animals wouldn't breed. People became hungry and violent, and many died. But once human blood was spilled once more and given to the land, the vineyard thrived and so did the community. Our collective well-being comes from our dependence on what lies beneath, and for that, we must give it blood."

Isabelle gestured around the chamber. "Every token here represents a life given, but countless more lives are improved. The money from the Blood Vintage supports the entire region. Schools, hospitals, conservation efforts, all funded by what we do here. The entire community is invested in ensuring a good harvest. Whatever it takes."

Rebecca could hardly take in the words, yet the truth of them resonated inside. There was something singular about this place, something ancient that she had glimpsed at times. It scared her and exhilarated her all at once, and to be so close to such a power must be intoxicating.

But Grace...

Rebecca stood. "I'm leaving now. I'll report this to the police, and the vineyard will be shut down. You'll go to jail. The community will pay for what you did to my sister, to Asha and Helen and Liam and all the others. It ends here. It ends now."

Isabelle rose to her feet and met the challenge in Rebecca's gaze.

She shook her head. "Who do you think protects us from the investigations that should have happened many times before? Standing Stone has close relationships with the police, the government, and those with the money to afford the Blood Vintage. Many of them were here for the party when Asha was sacrificed."

As the truth of Isabelle's words sank in, Rebecca stumbled towards the door. Of course, she couldn't be the first to discover this. Which meant that every other person had kept the vineyard's secret... or become part of the land in another way.

Isabelle reached out and clutched Rebecca's arm. "Wait, please."

Rebecca felt the strength in the older woman's grip and knew she would not make it out of the cellar if Isabelle determined it. She stopped and turned back.

"I have no daughter now," Isabelle said, a flicker of pain crossing her face. "She was called to the land too early, and the wild vines only accept a woman as guardian. I need someone strong to take my place, someone who understands how to keep the vineyard thriving. Someone to sit at the centre of our community. You fit in so well here, Rebecca, and I know you've heard the song of the vineyard. You could be the next guardian, and I will teach you the old ways... if you make this your home."

The offer hung in the air between them.

A tiny part of Rebecca, the part that had fallen in love with Standing Stone, desperately wanted to say yes. This was her home, and nowhere was ever perfect. Perhaps she could accept the balance necessary for the vineyard to flourish.

But then she clutched Grace's pendant more tightly, and the shape of it reminded her of what had been lost, and how many families had lost a loved one to this dark practice.

She couldn't be a part of murder, even if it benefitted the community. She had to get out of here, but there was no way to make it safely away from the vineyard right now, even if she could get to Ben and ask for his help.

Isabelle took her silence as conflicting emotion. "I know it's a lot to take in, but I'm not asking for an answer right now. Stay with us until Samhain. Join our most sacred ritual, drink our most precious wine, and your mind will open to the possibilities. Please, Rebecca, look how far you've come and consider what you could do here. Don't throw it all away now."

Rebecca took a step back. "And if I try to leave before then?"

Isabelle's smile was sad but determined. "I think we both know that's not an option. Stay for Samhain. It's only next week, and if you still want to leave after that, you can. No one will believe your story out there anyway, but you will be free to go, I promise. I give you my word."

Every fibre in Rebecca's body screamed that she was in grave danger, that she should run now and never look back or they would drag her out in the night and pound her bones and blood into the earth.

But even if she could escape, where would she go? Who would believe her story?

And deep down, a part of her she didn't want to acknowledge was intrigued. She was curious to see the ritual Isabelle spoke of and to understand the full extent of how Standing Stone Cellars imbued its wine with such power. Once she was through those ancient gates, would she be able to sense Grace's spirit?

"Alright," Rebecca heard herself say, as if from a great distance. "I'll stay until Samhain."

Isabelle's face lit up with genuine joy. She leaned forward and hugged Rebecca, who stood stiffly in her embrace. "You won't regret this. You've already heard the song of the vineyard and on the night when the veil is thinnest, I know you'll see a future for yourself here, and you will want to join us."

Together they walked back out of the wine cellar, and once up in the Manor House, Isabelle acted as if everything were normal. She took the key back to the library and Rebecca walked out into the afternoon.

The sounds of the labourers still came from the fields, the birds still sang, and machinery clanked from the processing area. Everything was normal, and yet everything had changed.

As she walked back to the shared bathrooms to clean her face, Rebecca saw Ben hard at work in the fermentation shed. He was bent over to work on a pump and didn't see her.

She could go to him right now, and together they could leave and expose it all, get justice for her sister and the others. But it would put him in danger, and given how many in the community were deeply enmeshed in the life of the vineyard, it was unlikely they would make it out of the area alive.

Besides, a dark curiosity had blossomed inside her, and Rebecca was determined to see what lay in the ancient heart of the vineyard. If she told Ben, she would never get to see it. She turned away and hurried on by.

CHAPTER 29

THE FINAL DAYS OF harvest passed quickly as the winery hummed with the constant movement of labourers and machinery. Rebecca threw herself into her work with a desperate intensity, hoping that the physical labour and mental focus would keep her tumultuous thoughts at bay.

She rose before dawn, her body moving on autopilot as she dressed and made her way to the fields. The morning air was crisp now with an autumn chill, and as she walked between the rows of late harvest vines, her breath formed small clouds that dissipated in the pale pre-dawn light.

Most of the vineyard now stood in stark contrast to the lush abundance of just weeks before. The once-verdant rows now resembled regimented lines of wooden sculptures, each vine a unique work of gnarled and twisted art. A few remaining leaves clung stubbornly to the vines, their colours transformed by the cooling temperatures and shortened days. What had been uniform green was now a patchwork of gold, russet, and burgundy. Some leaves spiralled in the air as Rebecca passed, launching on the wind to find their place in the cycle of the vineyard year.

Most of the remaining workers were on jobs in the winery, but a few moved methodically through the rows, carefully removing any leftover grape debris to prevent disease in the coming year. Others gathered fallen leaves and pruned canes, piling them high in trailers to be composted and eventually returned to nourish the soil.

Nate oversaw the application of specialised biodynamic sprays, although he didn't ask Rebecca to help with the preparations this time.

The fine mist from the sprayers caught the early light, creating ephemeral rainbows that danced between the rows.

"Remember," Nate instructed, his voice carrying in the still morning air, "we spray preparation 500 on the soil now to stimulate root growth and microbial activity. The 501 goes on when growth resumes in spring to enhance photosynthesis."

Nate didn't acknowledge that he knew of her discovery and her conversation with Isabelle, but in his guarded smile and forced small talk, Rebecca could tell he disapproved of Isabelle's decision to keep her close. As she watched his strong capable hands readying a backpack sprayer with a new mixture, she couldn't help wondering how many deaths Nate had been responsible for. She shivered a little at how much danger she might be in, now she was only here under Isabelle's protection. But that protection might not last too much longer, depending on what happened at Samhain.

The days passed and, in the equipment sheds, the constant clank and whir of machinery being cleaned and maintained provided a mechanical counterpoint to the more organic rhythm of the vineyard.

The vehicles and equipment were serviced, blades sharpened, and engines tuned in preparation for the winter pruning to come. The massive grape presses and fermentation tanks were meticulously scrubbed and sanitised, ready for their long rest until the next harvest.

After one morning shift in the vineyard, Rebecca retreated to the administration block to work on finalising her plans for the vineyard's expansion. The irony of continuing the work wasn't lost on her, but maintaining normalcy seemed her best chance of making it to Samhain unscathed.

Besides, a small, traitorous part of herself still thrilled at the organic beauty of her designs, and as she sat at the computer, inputting the last of the modifications requested by the council planning committee, Rebecca couldn't help but feel a sense of pride. The designs were the culmination of so many years of her experience and private study, her mastery of art and science blending seamlessly with the existing landscape while pushing the boundaries of sustainable architecture.

Living walls covered in native plants would provide natural insulation, while rainwater catchment systems would reduce the vineyard's reliance on external water sources. The new tasting room was a masterpiece of biophilic design, with floor-to-ceiling windows that dissolved the boundary between inside and out, allowing visitors the sense that they sat amongst the vines as they drank.

"These are really quite remarkable." Isabelle's voice came from behind her, causing Rebecca to start. She hadn't heard the older woman approach.

Rebecca forced a smile. "Thank you. I think they capture the essence of Standing Stone's uniqueness now while moving us into the future."

Isabelle nodded as she scanned the screen. "Indeed they do. You have a genuine gift, and I hope you'll stay on to oversee the construction once the plans are approved."

Rebecca swallowed hard, her throat suddenly dry. "Of course," she managed. "I'd love to see the project through to completion."

As Isabelle walked away, Rebecca turned back to her computer, her hands shaking slightly as she saved her work.

She had poured her heart and soul into these designs, and under different circumstances, she would have been excited at the prospect of seeing them come to life. But now, they felt like a seductive cage, designed to trap her in this place of exquisite beauty and ancient horror.

In the days since her discovery of the cabinet, Rebecca found herself almost constantly aware of Ben's presence. He worked tirelessly on repair and maintenance, and she often caught glimpses of him as he crossed the yard, his muscular arms glistening with sweat as he hefted crates of fruit or worked on the massive concrete steel tanks.

Part of her longed to tell him everything she had discovered, and together, they could escape this place.

But fear held her back.

Fear for his safety, and fear of what she might lose if she fled before Samhain. The curiosity that had taken root in her mind grew stronger with each passing day, a dark bloom unfurling in the shadows of her consciousness.

So she kept her distance, averting her eyes whenever their paths crossed, ignoring the hurt and confusion that flickered across Ben's face. It was safer this way, she told herself. Safer for both of them.

But her fears didn't stop when she closed her eyes. Visions of the Horned God plagued her dreams as the shadowy figure with mutated antlers watched her from the shadows of the vineyard, as if claiming her life for his own before she had the choice to offer it willingly.

As she resisted him, the surrounding vines came alive, writhing and twisting like serpents. They slithered through the windows of the bunkhouse and snaked across the floor. Rebecca tried to scream, desperate to escape, but her body remained paralysed as the tendrils wound their way up the bed frame, coiling around her limbs, pinning her to the mattress with inexorable strength.

As she struggled, gasping for air, the leafy tendrils circled her neck and began to squeeze even as they thrust down her throat, choking her.

At the edge of darkness, Rebecca woke, drenched in cold

sweat, her heart pounding. The Horned God was denied his sacrifice — at least for now — but the nightmares left her shaken.

One night, she couldn't sleep at all, for fear of what might take her while she lay unconscious.

She dressed quietly and wandered out into the vine rows.

In the pale moonlight, the landscape was otherworldly, as if she had stepped into a liminal space between reality and dream, where the veil was torn between this world and what lay beyond.

She stood amongst the rows, her bare feet sinking into the cool earth, and closed her eyes.

The night air carried the scent of fallen leaves and distant wood smoke, mingling with the aroma of fermentation from the winery. As she breathed deeply, Rebecca sensed the slow pulse of the land beneath her feet, the ancient rhythm that had drawn humans to this place for millennia.

A sense of belonging washed over her, so profound it almost brought tears to her eyes.

This was where she was meant to be. This land, this vineyard, it was all part of her now, just as she was a part of it.

She reached for Grace's pendant, which now hung around her own neck. Her sister understood this connection to the natural world and revelled in the old ways. Rebecca smiled to think that Grace would have loved her architectural designs and the changes she had made in her life, which benefitted her health and happiness, as well as the community.

Rebecca walked deeper into the vineyard, her feet sinking into the cool, damp earth with each step. The night air was crisp and still, carrying the autumn scent of decaying leaves and the earthy musk of fungi sprouting in hidden corners. The silence was broken by rustling leaves in the hedgerows from burrowing creatures and the distant hoot of a hunting owl.

The surrounding vines, though bare now, had stood for

generations. They had witnessed countless harvests, and watched generations of workers come and go as their roots delved deeper into soil enriched by years of growth and decay. Against this backdrop of enduring nature, a single human life was a fleeting spark, a brief flicker of light against the expanse of history.

Rebecca leaned against a sturdy vine post and gazed up at the star-strewn sky, pondering the vastness of time and the insignificance of human concerns.

Throughout history, people had always sacrificed to appease the gods, to ensure fertility and a good harvest, and to prevent disaster. Was Standing Stone just part of this ancient cycle?

If a few lives given could sustain an ancient power, provide wealth for a community, and produce something of transcendent beauty, wasn't that a fair exchange?

Rebecca tried to weigh the value of individual human lives against the enduring legacy of the vineyard, the jobs it provided, and the joy its wines brought to so many. As she walked amongst the vines, the scales of her mind tipped back and forth, unable to find a balance.

But then Grace's beautiful face flashed through her memory. Her sister's laugh, bright and clear. The weight of her arms in a sisterly embrace. A young life cut short, fed to the hungry earth beneath her feet.

Rebecca's steps faltered, and she sank to her knees in the cool dirt. She pressed her palms to the ground, trying to feel for some hint of Grace's presence, some justification for the loss. But there was only the quiet of the night and the faint stirring of the wind through the bare vines as she wept for her sister.

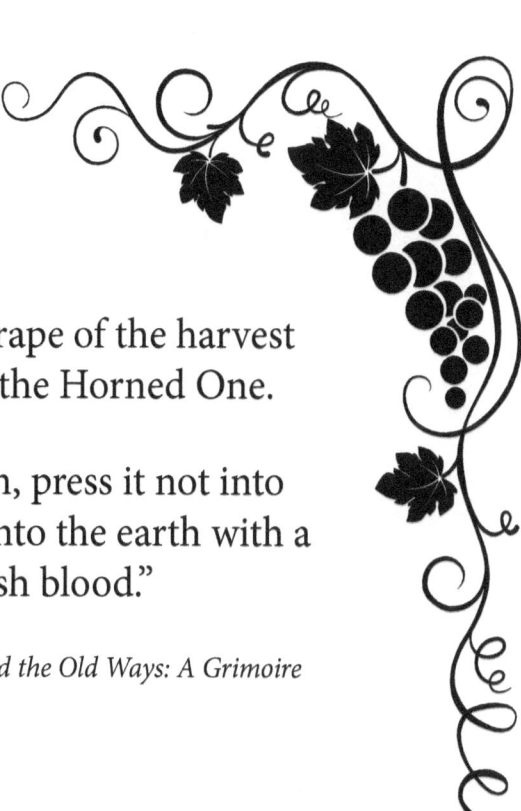

"The last grape of the harvest belongs to the Horned One.

At Samhain, press it not into wine, but into the earth with a drop of fresh blood."

—*Viticulture and the Old Ways: A Grimoire*

CHAPTER 30

As October progressed towards its end, the vineyard began to empty of its remaining seasonal workers. Each day, another group would depart, their laughter and chatter fading as they piled into cars or boarded buses bound for other harvests or winter jobs. Those who remained threw impromptu gatherings in the evenings, celebrating a successful season with music and, of course, plenty of wine.

Rebecca found it easy to lose herself in these celebrations, to pretend for a few hours that she was just another worker, happy and content in a job well done. But as the nights grew longer and Samhain drew nearer, a sense of unease settled over her.

The thinning of the workforce meant fewer people in the bunkhouses, fewer distractions from her thoughts. In the growing quiet, the whispers of the vineyard grew louder and more insistent.

On the last day of October, as the rays of sunlight faded from the sky, Standing Stone Cellars underwent a transformation to prepare for the celebration of Samhain.

Garlands of autumn leaves were strung between the vine rows in a vibrant tapestry of russet orange and gold, and the smell of wood smoke and rosemary hung in the air.

Carved turnip lanterns sat on top of posts, their grotesque faces illuminated from within by flickering candles. These were not the cheerful pumpkin lanterns of modern Halloween, but the original *samhnag* of Celtic tradition — fearsome guardians meant to ward off evil spirits on this night when the veil between worlds grew thin.

On the path to the manor house, bundles of wheat sheaves stood tied with red ribbons, symbols of the last harvest and the death of the old year. Offerings of apples and nuts were placed amongst them, traditional Samhain fare meant to honour the dead and appease the spirits of the land.

Behind the manor, close to the restricted area of ancient vines, a great bonfire had been built. It stood unlit for now, a towering pyre of seasoned logs and branches. This was the Tine Cnámh or 'bone fire' from which modern English derived the word bonfire. Traditionally, the fires in every hearth would be extinguished on Samhain, to be relit from this central sacred flame, symbolising unity and purification within the close-knit community.

A group of local women set up a table laden with food and drink. Small traditional soul cakes, some shaped like human figures, sat next to plates piled high with apples and nuts. Pitchers of mulled wine stood ready, the spiced aroma mingling with the smoke and herbs in the air.

Samhain was more than just a quaint harvest festival; it was a liminal time, a dangerous night when the boundaries between the world of the living and the realm of the dead became permeable. It was a time for honouring ancestors, divining the future, and making offerings to the spirits to ensure survival through the dark winter months ahead.

In agricultural communities like Winbridge Hollow, Samhain also marked the time when weak or sickly animals would be culled from the herd, unable to be sustained through the lean months ahead. A time of necessary sacrifice for the greater good of the community.

Rebecca suppressed a shudder as she considered how this ancient practice might have evolved into the darker rituals she was now aware of.

As twilight deepened into true night, Standing Stone workers and families from the village gathered, some with crowns of autumn leaves and others with antlers or animal masks, blurring the line between human and the wild spirits of nature.

A murmur ran through the crowd as the door of the manor house opened.

Isabelle emerged wearing an elaborate mask inspired by the maenads, the wild female followers of Bacchus. Rebecca caught her breath as she recognised the design from the book where she had found the key. Was Isabelle reminding her of her choice?

The mask was extraordinary, with twisted vines at the base, interwoven with clusters of ripe grapes fashioned from glass beads. Emeralds glinted among the foliage, catching the lantern light and reflecting it back like feline eyes in the dark. Isabelle was transformed into something more than human. She was a living embodiment of the vineyard's spirit, beautiful and terrible in equal measure.

Rebecca stood at the edge of the courtyard, gathering the strength to join in the celebrations. She wore a simple half-moon mask, crafted in honour of the biodynamic practices used at the vineyard. But it also represented the duality of her position, half in shadow, half in light. Caught between two worlds.

To be honest, she was still unsure whether her moon was waxing or waning, and which direction she would choose.

But time had run out.

Tonight she would make her choice and live — or die — by the consequences.

Rebecca felt a hand on her arm and turned to see Ben by her side.

He wore a red deer stag mask crafted from local ash wood. The antlers curved gracefully upward, giving him an air of natural nobility, but there was something in the set of his shoulders, and the way his eyes darted constantly around the gathering, that spoke of prey rather than predator.

"I know we haven't spoken much lately," Ben said softly. "But remember, I'm here if you need me."

"Thank you. I appreciate it." Rebecca touched his hand, her heart pounding as she almost gave in to the urge to tell him everything. If they escaped together right now while the community was engaged with the festival, perhaps they might see the dawn safely, away from this place.

Ben glanced over at Isabelle as she greeted the community. "Tonight is my last chance to find out the secrets of the ancient vines, and then I'm leaving tomorrow." He looked down at her, his eyes troubled. "Perhaps you'll come with me?"

Before Rebecca could answer, a loud, rhythmic drum beat rang out, echoing through the chill mist. The haunting melody of a tin whistle rose to meet it, weaving a mournful tune for the old year.

There was an energy in the air, like the electric atmosphere before a thunderstorm, the rumble in the distance before the sky splits open.

Isabelle led the community in a chant, with ancient words known by the old ones in a tongue long forgotten by the world outside this valley.

Once they chanted in unison, Isabelle sang above them in a keening melody that ignited something primal within Rebecca. She felt a sob rise up as some in the crowd wept and a sense of great tragedy pressed down upon them all.

This was not music for celebration, but for supplication. A plea for mercy.

Nate stepped forward with a flaming torch in his hand. He wore the mask of the Green Man, with a face both beautiful and terrifying. The dark, polished wood had been intricately carved to resemble gnarled vine branches that twisted and curled around his face. Small, lifelike leaves sprouted from wooden tendrils, and clusters of tiny grapes hung heavy around the eyeholes, so Nate could see through. Its mouth gaped open in a silent scream, either through the pain of transformation from man to vine, or to devour that which came close enough to it.

As Nate approached the unlit pyre, the chanting grew louder, more insistent.

He circled the great stack of wood three times; with each circuit, he lowered the torch to the ground at cardinal points, leaving trails of fire in his wake.

On the final pass, Nate paused at the eastern point of the circle. He raised the torch high above his head and called out, "We stand at the threshold of worlds at the dying of the year. We call upon the Horned God and the spirits of our ancestors. Bear witness to our rite, accept our offering, grant us your protection through the dark days to come."

With these words, he plunged the torch into the base of the pyre.

The fire caught quickly, racing up the carefully stacked wood until the entire structure was engulfed in flame.

The sudden blaze pushed back the darkness, casting flickering shadows across the faces of the gathered crowd.

Isabelle stepped forward, her maenad mask gleaming in the dancing light, a small cup in her hand.

She walked slowly around the perimeter of the fire, scattering herbs and small bones into the flames. With each addition, the fire flared with different colours — purple, green, and a blue so dark it was almost black.

"The bone fire burns," she intoned, her voice carrying clearly over the crackling flames. "The old year dies. The new year will be born from its ashes. Let all who dwell in the shadow of Standing Stone be renewed by its sacred flame."

Members of the community stepped forward, each picking up an unlit candle from a pile near the fire.

One by one, they approached and lit their candles from its flames before stepping back to form a great circle around the blaze.

The arc of light grew, spreading out from the central fire like the ripples from a stone cast into still water, a dance of shadow and flame that further blurred the boundaries between modern days and ancient times.

Rebecca joined the community and lit her own candle, finding her lips moving with one of the ancient prayers she recognised from the grimoire. Isabelle smiled at her with approval, and Rebecca felt the weight of her blessing.

Behind her, Ben also lit his candle, his expression hidden under his deer mask.

As the last candle was lit, the assembled community began to move, circling the fire in a slow, rhythmic dance. Their feet stamped out a primal beat on the earth as they swayed almost as one, their voices rising in the ancient chant that bound them together.

Rebecca found herself swept up in the movement, her body responding to the rhythm almost against her will. The heat of the fire, the swirling motion of the dance, and the hypnotic chanting all combined to create a dizzying, trance-like state.

After the third circle, Isabelle and Nate broke apart and stood before the great gates that led to the restricted area of ancient vines.

In the flickering light of the bone fire, the gates loomed larger than ever, a foreboding presence that pulsed with barely contained energy. The weathered wood, black with

J.F. PENN

age and stained with patches of lichen, bore the scars of countless seasons. Intricate carvings of spiralling faces and the symbols of the Horned God, worn smooth by time and countless hands, adorned the surface.

Heavy iron bands, mottled with rust, reinforced the ancient wood, and the hinges looked more suited to a medieval fortress than a vineyard. At the centre where the two gates met, a lock of curious design held them fast. Not a modern mechanism, but something older, a twisted amalgamation of metal that looked almost organic in its complexity.

The assembled crowd held its breath as Isabelle and Nate placed their hands on the gates and bent their heads to pray before pushing with all their strength.

Anticipation rose and Rebecca felt almost light-headed as she willed the gates to open, desperate to see what lay beyond.

The night seemed to pause, waiting, and for a long, breathless moment, nothing happened.

Isabelle and Nate pushed together once more, and the gates swung open with a deep groan. It was the sound of a seal being broken, of something long contained being set free.

CHAPTER 31

THE ANCIENT GATES OPENED slowly, the weathered wood protesting against the movement as if reluctant to reveal the secrets within. Isabelle and Nate walked through, followed by the masked community.

Rebecca hesitated at the threshold, taking a deep breath as she considered her options.

This was the last chance she had to run and take Ben with her. But curiosity drew her on. She needed to know what happened here and perhaps to learn something of Grace's fate.

Clouds scudded across the face of the moon and the silvery light flickered and waned, casting the landscape before her into a tapestry of shadow.

It took a moment for her eyes to adjust, but as she walked on, Rebecca made out the heart of the vineyard.

The vines here were truly ancient, their gnarled trunks twisted into shapes that spoke of centuries of slow, patient growth. Some must date back to Roman times — perhaps even earlier. These were not neat, cultivated rows like the rest of the vineyard. Here, the vines grew wild and free, their branches reaching towards the sky and their roots spread across the earth.

Interspersed amongst the vines were trees with massive

trunks, their bark deeply furrowed and covered in a patch-work of lichen and moss. Their branches formed a canopy overhead, creating the sense of walking through a primordial forest rather than a vineyard.

Countless feet had trodden this path before her, and Rebecca could almost sense them in the shadows.

Ghostly figures flitted between the vines, tending the land as their ancestors had done for millennia. Roman soldiers, their armour glinting under a long-forgotten sun. Saxon farmers and medieval monks, their chants rising on the night air as they harvested grapes for sacramental wine. The land went on, far outlasting each generation.

The smell of smoke came from up ahead and Rebecca could finally see the standing stones, lit by a ring of flaming torches set in metal barrels.

The ancient monoliths formed a rough circle, with some stones easily twice her height and broader than she could wrap her arms around. Others were smaller and leaned at precarious angles, as if frozen mid-collapse.

In the centre of the circle stood a massive flat stone, an altar, stained dark with the residue of countless rituals.

The smoke from the torches and the great bone fire beyond the gates wafted through the vineyard, carrying an intoxicating blend of herbs and wood resin. Rebecca felt her head swim as she breathed in the heady aroma, and the world around her shifted, blurring the boundaries between earth and sky.

In the shifting smoke and flickering light, the masked faces of the community wavered and changed, as if they became the strange creatures they represented.

The chanting grew louder as the community circled the exterior of the stones and without conscious thought, Rebecca joined in, her voice blending seamlessly with the others. The ancient language felt natural on her tongue, and each syllable resonated deep in her bones.

As she breathed in the smoke, Rebecca could no longer tell where her body ended and the vineyard began. She was the soil, rich and dark, nurturing the roots of countless generations of vines. She was the gnarled trunk, weathered by centuries of sun and rain. She was the tender leaf unfurling in the spring and the sweet grape swelling with the essence of long summer days.

Tears welled up in her eyes as she thought of how Grace was part of this land, out of time now. In becoming one with it, she lived on here in this special place.

The masked community wound in and out of the standing stones and, as the chant ended, they gathered around the altar, their breath misting in the chill night air.

An expectant hush fell over the assembly.

Isabelle stepped forward, her maenad mask glinting in the flickering torchlight. In one hand, she held a simple wooden cup, weathered and stained. In the other, a bottle that made Rebecca's breath catch in her throat at the elaborate label with its skull motif.

The Horned God's Share.

She had seen bottles like it in the wine cellar and had heard whispers of its rarity and value.

Isabelle raised her arms, her voice ringing out clear and strong in the night air. "Horned One, spirit of earth and vine, hear our plea."

As she spoke, the air thickened and became charged with a dark energy. The ancient vines rustled and swayed, as if stirring to Isabelle's call.

"On this night, when the veil is thin, we renew our ancient pact. Blood for wine, life for life. It has always been, and so it must be."

Isabelle poured wine into the wooden cup, the liquid so dark it seemed to absorb the torchlight.

Raising the cup high, she intoned, "To the land, to the vines, to the cycle of death and rebirth that sustains us all."

She brought the cup to her lips and drank.

Nate stepped forward next, accepting the cup from Isabelle with a solemn nod. He, too, drank, and then others from the community approached the altar.

One by one, they sipped from the cup as Isabelle refilled it with the precious wine.

Rebecca watched, transfixed. The ritual unfolding before her was primal, visceral in a way that bypassed her rational mind and spoke directly into something deep within her. She felt pulled forward, overcome by an almost overwhelming urge to be part of this. To taste the wine that was the heart and soul of Standing Stone.

She took a step forward, only to feel a hand grasp her arm.

Ben tried to pull her back, his eyes wide behind his stag mask. "No," he whispered urgently. "It's too dangerous."

For a moment, Rebecca hesitated.

Grace's beautiful face flashed through her memory, a reminder of all she had lost.

But then her gaze was drawn back to the cup and the dark liquid that promised… what? Understanding? Belonging?

Power.

Rebecca shook off Ben's grip. "I have to know," she said, her voice sounding strange and distant to her own ears. "I have to taste it."

She approached the altar with measured steps. Isabelle turned to her, the maenad mask tilted in what might have been a smile.

With a gesture of solemn gravity, she offered the cup.

Time slowed as Rebecca raised the cup to her lips. The scent hit her first — rich, complex, heady. Earth and sky, sun-warmed grapes and the cool, dark heart of what lay beneath the land.

The wine touched her tongue, a mere whisper at first.

It was layered, complex, a liquid embodiment of terroir.

A deep, rich blackcurrant melded seamlessly with hints of old wood and subtle undertones of strange herbs that grew in the shadowed parts of this forbidden sanctuary.

Beneath the dark fruit and earthy notes, there was something wilder — a feral, almost savage tang that spoke of hidden glades and secret groves, places untouched by human hands for millennia. Each drop was a distillation of centuries, capturing the essence of growth, decay, and rebirth that defined the vineyard's long history and every person who gave their life for it.

The warmth of the wine spread beyond Rebecca's throat, igniting a slow burn that felt less like drinking and more like descending into a deeper state of consciousness. It was seductive, intoxicating, and awakened within her a desperate craving for more.

All too soon, the last drops passed Rebecca's lips.

The cup was empty, but the craving remained — a visceral, almost painful desire that threatened to overwhelm her. She stared at the bottle in Isabelle's hand, almost ready to snatch it away, so desperate was her need for more of that transcendent liquid.

In that moment, Rebecca understood the true power of the blood vintage. It was more than just wine. It was a sacrament, a communion with something vast and ancient and terrible, and in its presence, she was nothing.

Isabelle gently but firmly removed the cup from Rebecca's grasp, her eyes gleaming with triumph beneath the mask.

Rebecca stumbled back to her place in the circle, her mind reeling with a sense of loss that almost broke her open, so desperate was she for more.

A drum beat shattered the silence, its deep resonance echoing through the ancient vineyard. It was joined by another, and another, building slowly into a hypnotic rhythm that pulsed in time with the earth beneath their feet.

The community circled the altar, some moving in their

animal guises, others raising their hands to the sky. Rebecca found herself beside Ben, his stag mask turned towards her.

He reached for her hand, but she pulled away, unable to bear the touch of his skin against hers. He had not tasted the wine, and that felt wrong, disrespectful, as if his presence was now an intrusion on the profound connection she felt with the land and the community.

"What was it like?" he whispered, his voice barely audible above the growing drum beat.

Rebecca opened her mouth to respond, but found she had no words to describe the experience. He had rejected any chance of understanding.

She shook her head, turning away from his concern.

The music quickened, the drums joined now by the wail of pipes and the jangle of tambourines. The masked celebrants moved, their bodies swaying and twisting in time to the primal rhythm.

Rebecca felt the beat in her bones, an irresistible call to join the dance. Without a backward glance at Ben, she threw herself into the whirling mass of bodies.

The smoke from the torches swirled around her, further blurring the lines between reality and some deeper, more primordial state of being.

She danced with abandon, guided by the music and the pulsing energy of the gathered community. Faces flashed by, masked and mysterious, each one a reflection of the power that flowed through this place.

The music built to a fevered pitch as dancers whirled faster and faster.

Suddenly a new sound cut through the night — the deep, resonant call of a horn.

As it came again, the wild dance slowed and then stopped.

The drum beat settled into a slow, ominous rhythm.

The masked celebrants gathered once more around the stone altar and an expectant hush fell over the gathering.

Rebecca pushed through to the front of the group, her breath coming in short gasps, her skin flushed with exertion and a dark anticipation.

But as she caught sight of the altar, the world tilted. She stumbled as she let out a cry.

Ben was bound tightly to the ancient stone, stripped naked, vulnerable in the flickering torchlight.

The stag mask still covered his face, its antlers now a cruel mockery of strength and nobility. His neck was bared while his mouth had been stuffed with vine leaves, silencing his cries.

He writhed against his bonds, the leather straps creaking as he struggled. But his efforts were futile — he was securely fastened, spread-eagled across the altar.

Rebecca couldn't look away from him, his muscles taut as they strained against his bonds. Ben was a perfect specimen of a healthy man in his prime, and she shivered at the memory of his body over hers in the rainstorm. He was a worthy sacrifice, and he would betray the community if he was allowed to go free.

She bit her lip in anticipation of what must come.

A torch flickered nearby and Rebecca felt herself suddenly thrust out of the strange trance she was in.

This was wrong.

This was Ben. Her friend, her lover. The only one who could help her reveal the truth of what happened here.

But as she tried to step forward, Rebecca felt hands on her shoulders, her arms, her back. The community pressed close, constraining her with their grip.

They whispered ancient prayers of supplication to whatever dark powers watched over this place, and Rebecca once again found the words rising unbidden to her lips. She knew these prayers, and now she understood their terrible purpose.

Her voice joined the chorus, blending seamlessly with

the others until she could no longer distinguish her words from those of the community.

Isabelle stepped forward, her maenad mask a reminder of the ecstatic and terrible rites of ancient times.

In one hand she held a full cup of The Horned God's Share and in the other a ritual knife, its hilt adorned with twisting vines carved from dark wood. The wickedly sharp blade caught the light of the flaming torches and reflected it, making her mask come alive with fire as she spoke.

"Blood for wine, life for life. It has always been, and so it must be."

Rebecca couldn't keep her gaze from that cup of wine, anticipating the taste that must surely come once blood had been spilled.

The world around her faded away, narrowing to that single point of focus. Her mouth went dry, her tongue sticking to the roof of her mouth as she imagined the rich, complex flavour.

Her skin crawled, a thousand tiny pinpricks of sensation racing across her body. It was as if every nerve ending had come alive, screaming out for the wine's touch. She could almost feel the liquid sliding down her throat, igniting a fire in her core that spread outward to her fingertips.

Her mind recoiled, torn by the danger lurking in that cup, but a primal part of her craved it with every fibre of her being. What hidden truths might be revealed if she could just have another taste?

Rebecca's hands trembled, and she clenched them into fists at her sides to hide the shaking. Her breath came in short gasps, her chest tight with longing.

She would give anything, do anything, for just one more sip.

Isabelle gave a feral smile as she met Rebecca's gaze. "Performing the sacrifice seals the bond between guardian and vineyard, and tonight, the Horned God summons another to take my place."

A gasp rose from the community as Isabelle held out the knife — and offered it to Rebecca.

She felt the pressure of their collective gaze, the weight of expectation. She stood on a precipice, teetering between two worlds. The life she had known — an ordered world of clear moral lines, right and wrong, justice and retribution. On the other side, the seductive draw of power, of belonging, of being part of something greater than herself — and the chance to drink once more.

The knife glinted in Isabelle's hand, its edge hungry for blood.

The air in the ancient grove grew thick, charged with dark energy as Ben's muffled struggle grew more frantic, his eyes wide with fear behind the stag mask.

The drum beat pulsed once more, a steady rhythm that matched the thundering of Rebecca's heart as she walked slowly to the altar, meeting Isabelle's gaze.

She reached out to take the knife.

CHAPTER 32

THE HANDLE OF THE blade was warm from Isabelle's touch and the knife felt lighter than Rebecca had expected, as if it belonged to her.

In these last months, she had found a home here — had been welcomed into communal practices like placing the frost candles, dew dancing with Isabelle, and harvesting grapes by moonlight with other women. She had celebrated ancient festivals and designed for the future of the vineyard.

It could be her future, too. She only had to take this last step.

Rebecca adjusted her grip, mirroring how Isabelle had held the knife when butchering the stag months ago. This would be no different and this body would feed the community as the stag had done.

She placed a hand on Ben's chest and then drew it up to his neck, feeling for his pulse.

Isabelle spoke once more. "Blood for wine, life for life. It has always been, and so it must be."

The community's chant grew louder, more insistent, and the drum beat matched the frantic pace of Rebecca's heart.

She lowered the blade to Ben's neck.

He stopped struggling, his body lying limp against the unyielding stone of the altar. But she could see his eyes, visible through the holes of the stag mask, and they looked at her with a silent plea.

Rebecca pressed the knife into his flesh, raising a single drop of blood.

A chill wind swept through the vineyard, whirling leaves from the ground, battering the community as an eerie moan echoed around the Standing Stones.

In that echo, Rebecca heard a single word.

Grace.

In that split second, she saw the future stretching out before her. Years of harvest ritual, of pleasure taken and power given, at the heart of this community.

But she also saw the cost. The lives sacrificed by her hand and the blood needed to renew the vines year after year.

She looked down, and instead of Ben's face, she saw her sister. A sacrifice to an ancient evil whose thirst for blood would never be quenched.

Unless someone broke the cycle.

She reversed the knife; instead of plunging it into Ben's flesh, she sliced through his bonds, releasing him.

"No!" Isabelle cried out.

The chanting and the drums faltered. For a heartbeat, the assembled community stood frozen in shock.

Chaos erupted.

Ben seized the moment of confusion and rolled off the altar. His mind and body were alert and fast, not slowed by the wine fogging the others.

He ripped off his mask, narrowly avoiding Nate's grasping hands, the older man's fingers closing on empty air where Ben had been just seconds before.

A collective gasp rose from the crowd, a sound of disbelief and dawning anger. Rebecca and Ben had only moments before the shock wore off and the full fury of the thwarted ritual was turned upon them.

Rebecca reached over to Isabelle and lashed out, her

hand connecting with the bottom of the cup.

The precious wine, a product of centuries of dark ritual and terrible sacrifice, arced through the air in a glittering spray. It splashed across the ground, soaking into the dry leaves and grass that carpeted the ancient heart of the vineyard.

The solemn chant of moments ago gave way to screams of panic and rage.

Some of the community fell to their knees, lapping at the drops of wine with abandon while others advanced on the offenders, their eyes glinting with murderous intent behind their masks.

Rebecca and Ben each grabbed one of the flaming torches that ringed the standing stones.

Ben swung his in a wide arc, keeping the community back as they advanced in a feral horde. If they remained here, they would both be sacrificed, ripped apart in anger at their trespass.

There was only one choice.

Rebecca turned and knocked over the barrel holding another torch, sending flames and burning embers into the litter of dry leaves tucked against the vine trunks.

The first spark caught and spread quickly. The vines, their wood dry and gnarled with age, caught like tinder.

Flames raced up their twisted trunks, leaping from vine to vine as the air filled with the acrid scent of burning wood.

The massive old tree at the centre of the grove, its branches reaching towards the star-strewn sky, became a colossal torch. The flames engulfed it from root to crown, turning its ancient wood into a pillar of fire that lit up the night like a vengeful sun.

The community tried to stop the growing fires from spreading, but they were uncoordinated and clumsy, moving too slowly under the influence of the wine to make a difference.

Through the chaos, Rebecca heard Isabelle's voice rise above the din. The older woman's usual composure had shattered, replaced by shrill desperation as she shouted orders to the panicking crowd.

"Save the vines!" she screamed.

Ben grabbed Rebecca's arm. "We have to go. Now!"

They turned and fled, pushing through the ring of attackers as hands grasped at them, trying to hold them back.

But the press of bodies worked against the community now, and in the confusion of billowing smoke, Rebecca and Ben slipped through.

The heat was intense, stealing the breath from their lungs. Flames licked at their heels as they ran. The fire spread, cutting off paths and herding them away from the gates.

"This way!" Ben yelled, pulling Rebecca towards a gap in the flames.

They ran on blindly, smoke stinging their eyes as the landscape became a maze of blazing wood and falling fiery embers.

A burning branch crashed down in front of them, sending up a shower of sparks. Rebecca stumbled, nearly falling, but Ben's grip on her arm kept her upright.

They veered sharply, taking a new path through the inferno.

The sounds of pursuit came from behind. Shouts and screams echoed through the burning vineyard, some close, others more distant.

The smoke thickened, making it hard to breathe. Rebecca's lungs burned, and every breath was a struggle.

She could feel her strength flagging, her legs growing heavier with each step. Beside her, she could hear Ben's laboured breathing.

"We can't… keep this up," he gasped between breaths. "We need… to find… a way out."

Rebecca nodded, unable to spare the breath for words. It

couldn't be far, but which way to go? The fire seemed to be everywhere, consuming the vineyard with unnatural speed and hunger. Had they merely traded one death for another, escaping sacrifice only to burn?

A gust of wind suddenly parted the smoke and through the gap, Rebecca glimpsed the high fence that marked the boundary of the restricted area. Beyond it lay the main part of the vineyard, as yet untouched by the flames, and there, the great doors remained open.

Their way out.

As they ran towards it, screams of fear and pain rose out of the fire behind them.

Rebecca hesitated and looked back. Through gaps in the wind-whipped smoke, she could see figures stumbling through the inferno, their elaborate costumes now nothing more than kindling.

For a moment, she wanted to turn back and help the community. These were people she had worked alongside for months, people she almost considered family, who had changed her life for the better in so many ways.

"We have to get out." Ben grabbed her hand and pulled her on. "It's too late. We can't save them!"

She knew he was right. The fire was too intense, and spreading too quickly. To go back would be suicide.

They ran out of the gate and into the courtyard, where the bone fire had burned down to cinders. It lay constrained by stones which controlled its reach even as the wildfire raged out of control beyond the ancient wooden staves.

Rebecca's legs gave out, and she sank to her knees in the courtyard as the adrenaline that carried her through their escape faded, leaving her shaky and nauseous.

Ben knelt next down and pulled her close as the flames rose into the sky.

Other figures emerged from the smoke-filled gateway. Community members, their elaborate costumes now tattered and singed, stumbled out into the relative safety of the main vineyard.

They coughed and retched, faces streaked with soot and eyes wide with shock and disbelief as they wandered out into the night. They ignored Rebecca and Ben as if the fire had broken the spell of The Horned God's Share.

A movement near the heart of the fire caught Rebecca's eye and her gaze was drawn inexorably back to the blazing heart of Standing Stone Cellars.

Isabelle stood in the heart of the flames, the burned body of Nate at her feet. Her maenad mask was gone and her silver hair whipped around her face like a fiery crown. She stood tall and proud, a living embodiment of the vineyard's ancient power, as the fire licked her flesh.

Their eyes met across the gulf of flame and smoke and Rebecca saw a flicker of emotion cross Isabelle's face — sorrow, perhaps, or it could have been relief. Her bond had been broken, not in the way she had expected, but at last, the guardian of the vineyard would join her family under the earth.

As the flames took her, Isabelle raised her hand in what might have been a blessing. She sank to her knees and then to the ground.

A deep, mournful sound rose above the crackling of flames, the death cry of something ancient and terrible as the Horned God, the spirit of the vineyard, burned along with his vines and those who served him.

As the melancholy cry echoed into the night, Rebecca wept for Grace and for Isabelle and all those caught in the vineyard's dark embrace. And she wept for herself, for the burden of knowledge she now carried. For the life that might have been.

EPILOGUE. FIVE YEARS LATER

THE OCTOBER SUN HUNG low in the sky, casting long shadows across the scarred landscape of what had once been Standing Stone Cellars. The air was crisp, carrying the scent of fallen leaves and damp earth, and a gentle breeze whispered through the skeletal remains of charred vines.

Emma Thorne paused at the crest of the hill, one hand resting protectively on her swollen belly. At seven months pregnant, she found herself easily winded, especially on the uneven terrain of their newly acquired property. Her husband, James, stood a few paces ahead, surveying the land with a mixture of excitement and trepidation.

"It's hard to believe no one wanted this place," Emma said once she caught her breath. "I mean, I know the history is… complicated. But there's so much potential here."

James nodded, a smile playing at the corners of his mouth. "Most people can't see past the tragic deaths, or the ridiculous rumours of pagan blood rituals. All they see is superstition and destruction."

He bent down and scooped up a handful of dark soil, crumbling it between his palms. "But where others see an ending, we can start again. It's a new beginning. After fire comes renewal. It's the cycle of nature."

Emma took his hand, mingling the soil between their

entwined fingers. "What kind of place will we build?" She put a hand on her belly. "What will this little girl see as she runs around in a few years' time?"

James gestured over the fields before them. "A vineyard that respects the land and works in harmony with nature rather than trying to dominate it. We'll use sustainable practices, and maybe even biodynamic methods, as the last vineyard owners did. We'll create wines that truly capture the essence of this place."

He turned and hugged her, his eyes alight with a vision of the future. "I can almost hear the land calling out for us, Em. It's desperate to be a place of abundance once more. We're meant to be here, to be part of its rebirth."

Emma smiled up at him. "We'll build it together, and our family can grow with it."

She pointed out the darkest patch of blackened vineyard below, behind what looked like the remnants of an ancient stave fence. "We haven't looked at that section yet."

They walked down the hill, picking their way slowly through the remnants of the old vineyard. Here and there, signs of life pushed through the ash-strewn earth, hardy weeds and even some late Michaelmas daisies.

At last, Emma and James reached the heart of the property, where a pair of massive gates lay fractured in pieces. The wood was charred and pitted, bearing the scars of the inferno that had swept through the vineyard years ago.

Emma reached out and touched the rough surface of the wood. "I read about this section in the property documents. It's the oldest part of the vineyard, dating back to Roman times. It was also the most damaged by the fire. Perhaps we'll have to fence it off and let it stay fallow for a few more years?"

James took a few steps beyond the gate.

A cloud passed over the sun, casting him into the gloom. For a moment, Emma thought she saw a horned shadow sliding from the darkness towards her husband.

She shivered at the sudden cold and reached out for him. "James, don't go in there. It might be dangerous, unstable."

He looked back. "I won't go far."

As he turned to walk on, something caught his eye, and he crouched to examine the ground.

James looked up, excitement in his eyes. "You have to see this, Em. Look, signs of life, even here."

Emma joined him, her arms around her belly against the bitter wind that swirled around them. She placed a hand on his shoulder to steady herself and looked down.

The tendril was unmistakably a grapevine, its leaves small but perfectly formed. It grew from a gnarled old root that must have survived the fire. It pushed up through the ash-covered soil with stubborn determination.

James smiled up at his wife. "If vines can survive here, in the heart of devastation, there's hope for the rest of the land. I can't wait to get started, Em."

As they walked back to their car, the sun dipped below the horizon, painting the sky with a crimson stain. The charred vines cast long shadows across the ground and the silhouette of a horned creature formed, watching, waiting for the sacrifice that must surely come once more.

AUTHOR'S NOTE

AS EVER, MY STORIES come from places I visit and this one starts much closer to home than usual. In the summer of 2023, I went on a wine tour at Woodchester Valley, a boutique vineyard in the Cotswolds, where I learned of the renaissance of English wines because of climate change. They mentioned a much older part of the vineyard which we couldn't visit, and my story instincts started twitching.

That night — perhaps under the influence of their delicious sparkling rosé — I remembered a performance of Euripides' *The Bacchae* that I attended back at school.

It was the early '90s, and I was around fifteen years old. I was studying Ancient Greek and Classical Civilisation at the time, and the performance was at an outdoor amphitheatre and in the Ancient Greek language. I've always had a strong imagination and watching the climactic scene in torchlight, as the feral horde ripped apart the sacrifice, has always stuck with me.

I previously explored the hungry power of nature in *Tree of Life*, which has a wild Eden at its heart. I wanted to revisit those themes again in a different way.

The vineyard visit also brought to mind an interview I did with vintner Caro Feely about her Chateau Feely vineyard in France. Amongst all the fascinating things we talked about, we discussed how dangerous a vineyard could be and how many ways there might be to die there. We're both authors, so that's a completely normal conversation! She also told me about biodynamics, where strange ingredients are buried to enrich the vines. Clearly, those ideas took root.

Around the same time, we watched *Drops of God (2023)* which has a deeply evocative exploration of viticulture from the perspective of two very different people who battle to win a valuable wine collection after the owner's death.

In terms of the folklore aspects, I live in Bath, Somerset, England, a short drive from Glastonbury, famed for its ancient sites and pagan practices. While the English may seem very proper and stiff-upper-lipped to Americans, we certainly have some darker rituals, and pagan festivals are still celebrated in this area. The Border Morris dancers at Beltane are modelled on The Dark Gathering, www.thedarkgathering.co.uk, who perform at such events.

The Horned God emerged during the writing process as I read more about the Wild Hunt. I also remembered things from my childhood that played a part.

Back in the '80s, we lived in Bristol, not far from where I live now, and the TV show *Robin of Sherwood*, starring Jason Connery, was filmed in Leigh Woods nearby. In my memory, we went to watch some of the filming and Herne the Hunter stepped out of the shadows and the smoke, a mysterious man/god with antlers like a deer. It's possible we never went to watch the filming as memory is unreliable, but the image of Herne the Hunter remained, regardless.

Around the same time, *The Box of Delights* was shown on TV and I will always remember 'the wolves are running,' and how this kind of wild nature terrified me. I was only nine or ten at the time!

Back to viticulture, we also have one of England's only biodynamic vineyards, Limeburn Hill Vineyard, within an hour's drive from my house. As part of my research, I did an Introduction to Biodynamic Winegrowing Workshop in June 2024, which was fascinating. While I have borrowed some of the setting and ideas from their biodynamic practices, Limeburn Hill is about as far from Standing Stone Cellars as you might expect! It is a wonderful place with kind and generous owners, and I highly recommend a visit — and of course, make sure you ask to see the place they bury the bones…

I also did a stone carving workshop that same summer and ended up with a Green Man who now sits in my garden amongst the petunias.

In the library, *Liber Ivonis* is a fictional grimoire of dark magic that appears in the works of H. P. Lovecraft and other writers of the Cthulhu Mythos. The title is Latin and translates to the Book of Ivon or Book of Eibon. I couldn't resist a Lovecraft callback!

I also found inspiration from the film *Midsommar* (2019) and the original 1973 movie *The Wicker Man*, as well as the folk horror novel *The Reddening* by Adam Nevill, one of my favourite horror authors.

Note on spelling. **Although most of my books use American English, I decided that, given the setting, this one should be British English.**

Bibliography and resources

"A Weekend Stone Carving" — and my Green Man — www.booksandtravel.page/stone-carving

Voodoo Vintners: Oregon's Astonishing Biodynamic Winegrowers — Katherine Cole

Limeburn Hill Biodynamic Vineyard, Chew Valley, England — www.limeburnhillvineyard.co.uk

My full day workshop and photos from Limeburn Hill: www.booksandtravel.page/limeburn-hill-biodynamic-vineyard

The Dark Gathering Morris dancers — www.thedarkgathering.co.uk

"The Taste of Place. French Vineyard Life with Caro Feely" — www.booksandtravel.page/vineyard

Woodchester Valley Vineyard, Stroud, England — www.woodchestervalleyvineyard.co.uk

ACKNOWLEDGEMENTS

Thanks to Christy Frank, Copake Wine Works, and Pauline O'Connor, www.PigPen.page, for the viticulture expertise.

Thanks to (Dr) Icy Sedgwick, author of *Rebel Folklore*, for folklore expertise: www.icysedgwick.com

Thanks to my editor Kristen Tate at The Blue Garret, and my book designer, Jane at JD Smith Design.

MORE BOOKS BY J.F. PENN

ARKANE Action-Adventure Thrillers

Stone of Fire #1
Crypt of Bone #2
Ark of Blood #3
One Day in Budapest #4
Day of the Vikings #5
Gates of Hell #6
One Day in New York #7
Destroyer of Worlds #8
End of Days #9
Valley of Dry Bones #10
Tree of Life #11
Tomb of Relics #12
[Stand-alone ARKANE story — Soldiers of God]
Spear of Destiny #13

Brooke and Daniel Psychological/Crime Thrillers

Desecration #1
Delirium #2
Deviance #3

Mapwalker Dark Fantasy Adventures

Map of Shadows #1
Map of Plagues #2
Map of the Impossible #3

Horror

Catacomb
Risen Gods
Blood Vintage

Short Stories

A Thousand Fiendish Angels
The Dark Queen
A Midwinter Sacrifice
Blood, Sweat, and Flame
With a Demon's Eye
Beneath the Zoo
De-extinction of the Nephilim

Travel Memoir

Pilgrimage:
Lessons Learned from Solo Walking Three Ancient Ways

More books coming soon …

You can sign up to be notified of new releases, giveaways and pre-release specials - plus, get a free ebook!

WWW.JFPENN.COM/FREE

If you loved the book and have a moment to spare, I would really appreciate a short review on the page where you bought the book.

Your help in spreading the word is gratefully appreciated and reviews make a huge difference to helping new readers find the series. Thank you!

ABOUT J.F. PENN

J.F. Penn is the Award-winning, New York Times and USA Today bestselling author of thrillers, dark fantasy, crime, horror, short stories, and travel memoir.

Jo lives in Bath, England and enjoys a nice G&T.

You can find my J.F. Penn Reading Order at:
www.jfpenn.com/readingorder

Buy books directly from me:

www.JFPennBooks.com

* * *

Sign up for your free thriller, Day of the Vikings, and receive updates from behind the scenes, research, and giveaways at:

WWW.JFPENN.COM/FREE

* * *

Connect with Jo:
www.JFPenn.com
Instagram @jfpennauthor
Facebook @jfpennauthor
X @thecreativepenn
www.BooksAndTravel.page

* * *

For writers:

Joanna's site, www.TheCreativePenn.com empowers authors with the knowledge they need to choose their creative future. Books by Joanna Penn, as well as her award-winning show, *The Creative Penn Podcast*, provide information and inspiration on writing craft and creative business.